While Monty was writing the cheque he
preserved a reverent silence, As as if fearing lest
the slightest interruption might be fatal, but
as soon as he had pocketed it he became his
garrulous self again.

'It probably strikes you as odd, my dear Bodkin, that a
man of my wealth should be borrowing money,
even from an old friend like you. The explanation can be
given in a word or, rather, two words. Joint account.'

'I beg your pardon?'

'My wife and I have a joint account.'

'Oh?'

'You say 'Oh' lightly, Bodkin, apparently not
recognising the significance of those two words.'

'You mean - ?'

'I mean that I can't write a check for the
smallest amount without having her ask 'What
the hell was this for?' I didn't know if she told
you that we were off for a few days to the South
of France?'

'Yes. To Cannes, she said.'

'Exactly. To Cannes, where the facilities
for gambling are unexampled. Roulette is
my game, Bodkie. I have a system that
can't fail. But if I drew a thousand pounds
from our London account and she asked me
what it was for and I said 'Playing roulette,'
she would ... well, she would express
herself very forcibly. My wife does not like
parting with money unnecessarily. So she
disapproves of playing at the casinos. It's
not the winning she objects to, but she would
hate to lose.'

The World of P. G. Wodehouse

Herbert Warren Wind

HUTCHINSON
London Melbourne Sydney Auckland Johannesburg

Hutchinson & Co. (Publishers) Ltd

An imprint of the Hutchinson Publishing Group

17-21 Conway Street, London, W1P 5HL

Hutchinson Group (Australia) Pty Ltd
30–32 Cremorne Street, Richmond South, Victoria 3121
PO Box 151, Broadway, New South Wales 2007

Hutchinson Group (NZ) Ltd
32–34 View Road, PO Box 40–086, Glenfield, Auckland 10

Hutchinson Group (SA) (Pty) Ltd
PO Box 337, Bergvlei 2012, South Africa

First published in Great Britain 1981

Printed in Great Britain by The Anchor Press Ltd,
and bound by Wm Brendon & Son Ltd,
both of Tiptree, Essex

British Library Cataloguing in Publication Data
Wind, Herbert Warren
   The World of P. G. Wodehouse.
   1. Wodehouse, P. G. – Criticism and
   interpretation
   I. Title
   823'.912   PR6045.053297

   ISBN 0–09–145670–3

For
John A. T. Sharp

Endpaper: manuscript pages from
Pearls, Girls and Monty Bodkin, published in
October 1972

Frontispiece: Wodehouse at 90.
Photograph by D. R. Bensen

⚊≡ I ≡⚊

Introduction

The basis of this study of P. G. Wodehouse is the series of weekly sessions I had with him in the winter of 1969–70 for the purpose of preparing a profile for the *New Yorker* magazine. During that December, January, February, and March, I would drive out on the appointed day – usually Wednesday – from New York to Remsenburg, a pleasant village some seventy-five miles away on the south shore of Long Island, where Wodehouse and his wife had made their full-time home since 1959. By that time they had known Remsenburg for almost twenty years, for Wodehouse's old and good friend Guy Bolton, with whom he had collaborated on many musical comedies, had lived there since 1941, and the Wodehouses had visited the Boltons often. In 1959 Wodehouse turned seventy-eight, and while he was still in excellent health and full of vigour, the pace of life in Remsenburg was very much to his tastes. As a young man he had relished the vitality of London and New York, but by 1959 he didn't think he was missing much in being deprived of the rush and roar of metropolitan life. He was eighty-eight the winter I got to know him.

There was a definite pattern to our weekly sessions. As a rule, I arrived at his home a little before eleven, and we talked together for about two hours. We never worked in his study, where he did his writing at an unfancy wooden desk and thought out his plots in a comfortable armchair. We met instead in the larger of the house's two sun parlours, a room with lots of windows facing south and west. At Wodehouse's suggestion, we used a tape recorder. He wanted our sessions to be relaxed and enjoyable, and he knew they wouldn't be if I kept interrupting the conversation to scribble down what he was in the process of saying. He usually sat at one end of a brightly covered sofa, smoking his pipe and holding one of the household dogs. Wodehouse was a gifted talker. He would take a moment to think before answering most questions, and when he spoke his sentences flowed as smoothly as a meadowland stream. He made no effort to be humorous or to come up with brilliant phrases, but frequently the events he was recalling would tickle him, and at these times his cheerful voice would brighten a discernible degree and he would become as amusing as he was on paper. For a man in his late eighties, his memory was exceptional. In fact, his mind was so supple and exact that one forgot completely about his age.

At one o'clock we would stop our work and drive to Westhampton Beach, about five miles away, for lunch. Wodehouse usually would call in first at the stationery shop on the main street to pick up his copy of *Variety*, long known in America as the 'Bible of Show Business'. He liked to keep up with what was happening in the theatre and in the other sectors of the entertainment world. Each week we lunched at the same restaurant, the Patio. The main room was large and not too attractive – the sort of overly spacious room where the local Rotary Club meets. The grill was much nicer. It was a cosy room with panelled wood walls and, I believe, red-and-white-checked tablecloths. Whenever he entered the grill, Wodehouse would light up like a schoolgirl being taken to lunch by a wealthy aunt or uncle. He got to eat out rarely in those days, for his wife did all the driving, and she preferred to take her meals at home or at their friends' homes. At the Patio he always started off with a bourbon sour. As he sipped it and took in the twenty or so people gathered in the grill in the quiet winter season, he would invariably say something along the lines of, 'This is just the kind of room I like. I say, isn't it pleasant here.' He always ate well and was full of good conversation, ranging from his views on Wilkie Collins' *The Moonstone* – he thought it was perhaps overpraised since 'only one person, really, could have stolen the stone' – to how much he had admired Nolan Ryan's pitching in the last weeks of the New York Mets' pennant drive in 1969 and subsequently in the World Series. He was a tremendous listener.

Some days, after we had driven back to Remsenburg, I headed directly back to New York if Wodehouse seemed drowsy. Other days, we would switch the tape recorder on again and do a little more work. Our afternoon sessions never lasted beyond three-fifteen, for at three-thirty each weekday he dutifully watched a television 'soap opera' called 'The Edge of Night'.

After I had finished writing the profile and had turned it in, I kept up with Wodehouse and went out to see him every so often. Early in 1971 I learned that the *New Yorker* was not planning to run the profile in the next few months. I wrote to Wodehouse and told him this disappointing news. I received his reply three or four days later. 'You mustn't worry too much about the delay in using the piece', he wrote. 'As a matter of fact, it would suit me if it was postponed till 15 October when – if I survive – I shall have my ninetieth birthday and a new Jeeves novel published. I am writing this in a hurry, as Ethel [Mrs Wodehouse] is straining at the leash to go to the post office to get the mail.'

The profile ran that spring in the issue of 15 May.

II

Chap with a Good Story to Tell

═ I ═

At seven-thirty sharp each spring or summer morning – in fact, just about every pleasant morning the year round – a tall, broad-backed, bespectacled eighty-nine-year-old resident of the peaceful Long island village of Remsenburg made it a practice to open the front door of his rambling cottage, step out on to the porch, and run through a series of twelve calisthenic exercises – the famous daily dozen, which were introduced in the United States in 1919, and which, from that year on, he did faithfully each day. When this task was completed, the octogenarian, his light-blue eyes and his bald head shining perceptibly brighter, would go back inside the cottage and, since the rest of the household had yet to arise, fix himself his regular breakfast of toast, coffee cake, and tea. He ate this at a leisurely tempo, spreading jam or marmalade or honey over the toast as he read a 'breakfast book' – either a mystery, on the order of Ngaio Marsh's *Dead Water*, or something light, like Russell Maloney's *It's Still Maloney*. By nine o'clock, having finished a pipeful of the shredded tobacco of a Dutch Masters cigar and taken a short walk with one or more of the family's four dogs, he moved eagerly to his study and got down to work on the novel or short story or article he was writing. The busy, methodical fellow was P. (for Pelham) G. (for Grenville) Wodehouse, the English-born humorist, who, as he approached ninety, continued to bring out at least one new book each year – a pace he had maintained since 1902, when his first novel, *The Pothunters*, was published.

One of the most prolific writers of all time, Wodehouse had by that time – 1971 – churned out seventy-odd novels, including nine about his two best-known characters, Bertie Wooster and his valet Jeeves; more than three hundred short stories, including some thirty about Wooster and Jeeves; and around five hundred sprightly essays and articles. In between, Wodehouse had found the time to publish a fairly large amount of humorous verse, to work on the scenarios of half a dozen motion pictures, to write, or collaborate in the writing of, sixteen plays, and to provide the lyrics for twenty-three musical comedies. The most impressive thing about this staggering output was its consistently high quality, and this attribute, so exceptional in the marshy field of humour, no doubt helps to explain the fervour of his large following. 'Temperate admirers of his work are non-existent', James Agate, the English drama critic, said of Wodehouse. 'Like O. Henry, this writer apparently divides the world into two classes – those who cannot read his books and those who can read no others.' The breadth of Wodehouse's appeal is also exceptional; down through the years, his hard-core fans have ranged from Bertrand Russell to Bix Beiderbecke, the great jazz cornettist, who could quote page after page from his stories. Herbert Asquith, during the difficult weeks that followed his defeat in 1918, found solace in reading Wodehouse, and two other British Prime Ministers, Arthur Balfour and Stanley Baldwin, were also ardent Wodehousians. (Balfour was especially enchanted by Wodehouse's dedication of *The Heart of a Goof*: 'To my daughter Leonora, without whose never-failing sympathy and encouragement this book would have been finished in half the time.')

In view of the pain it gives most writers to say a good word about other writers, perhaps the most eloquent testimonials to Wodehouse's talent are the warm compliments that have been paid him by colleagues, among them Rudyard Kipling, Agatha Christie, George Orwell, Malcolm Muggeridge, Peter Quennell, Ogden Nash, and Evelyn Waugh. In a foreword he supplied to a collection called *Nothing but Wodehouse*, published in New York in 1932, Nash declared, 'To inhabit the same world as Mr Wodehouse is a high privilege; to inhabit the same volume, even as a doorkeeper, is perilous.' Waugh, a notoriously hard man to please, happily confessed that he had grown up 'in the light of his genius', and added, 'I still await with an unappeasable appetite each addition to the *œuvre*.' In the early 1930s, Hilaire Belloc, the poet and critic, declared in a radio talk that Wodehouse was without qualification 'the best writer of English now alive'. This deeply offended Hugh Walpole, the novelist. After sulkily protesting against Belloc's evaluation for weeks in conversations with his friends, Walpole happened to run into Wodehouse, and asked him what in the world could have led Belloc to say a silly thing like that. Before Wodehouse could say a word, Walpole, answering his own question, suggested that maybe the explanation was that Belloc was getting on in years and obviously wasn't as sharp as he used to be. Wodehouse, ever the soul of courtesy, allowed that those were exactly his thoughts.

Whether or not Wodehouse deserved Belloc's tribute, he would undoubtedly receive the vote of many people in and around the literary world as the most outstanding humorist since Mark Twain. It is also more than likely that he has been the most widely read humorist since Twain. The exact figures on the sales of Wodehouse's books are not available, but people in a position to offer reliable estimates place the number between twenty and thirty million. While it is never easy to translate comic writing – and Wodehouse's heavy reliance on both English and American slang adds another dimension of difficulty – his books not only have been issued in French, Spanish, Portuguese, German, Dutch, Czech, Polish, Finnish, Norwegian, Swedish, Danish, Chinese, and Japanese but have done surprisingly well. Certainly few writers, comic or serious, have come close to Wodehouse's feat of maintaining an almost unbroken popularity for more than a half a century. In the late 1960s, his American publisher, Simon & Schuster, recognizing the evergreen appeal of his earlier books, inaugurated a series called the P. G. Wodehouse Classics by reissuing *Fish Preferred* (first published in 1929; its British title is *Summer Lightning*), *The Code of the Woosters* (1938), and *Uncle Fred in the Springtime* (1939).

The staying power and apparent universality of Wodehouse's work are all the more confounding when one reflects that he writes about a world as special, inbred, and remote as William Faulkner's Yoknapatawpha County, Thomas Hardy's Wessex, or J. R. R. Tolkien's Middle Earth. A number of Wodehouse's stories are specifically set in New York or Hollywood, in the period between the two world wars, and yet wherever and whenever the action takes place his world is Edwardian England. The pace of that world is slow. The big event coming up is the performance of Gilbert and Sullivan's *The Sorcerer* that the Choral Society will be giving in aid of the Church Organ Fund. There is occasionally a radio, but no television, and the object that the careless hand knocks off the mantelpiece is likely to be a plaster cast of the Infant Samuel at prayer.

The chief denizens of this world are agreeable idle-rich young men, the scions of aristocratic families, who wear morning coats and spats, and talk about avoiding 'rannygazoo' (unpleasant situations) and finding a girl who is absolutely 'oojah-cum-spiff' (perfection). They make their London headquarters at the Drones Club. (Bertie Wooster is a member of the Drones, and so are Bingo Little, Pongo Twistleton, Freddie Widgeon, Gussie Fink-Nottle, and Oofy Prosser, all of whom are fairly active members of the Wodehouse stock company. Names, by the way, were important to Wodehouse, and he was very good at concocting them.) In Wodehouse's world, mothers and fathers are almost never on the scene, and instead we have a proliferation of aunts and uncles. (Bertie Wooster has two aunts, Dahlia and Agatha. Stanley Featherstonehaugh Ukridge has an Aunt Julia. Pongo Twistleton has an Uncle Fred, who is Lord Ickenham. And so on.) When these young men are not in London, they are invariably spending long weekends at posh country houses, visiting relatives or friends. (These country houses have names like Skeldings, Tudsleigh, Brinkley Court, Totleigh Towers, and Matcham Scratchings. The poshest of them is Blandings Castle, the home of the ninth Earl of Emsworth. A nice, woolly-headed old fellow, Lord Emsworth is at or near the centre of the action in twelve novels and twenty-odd short stories.)

It is rare for one of Wodehouse's young men not to be deeply involved with a young lady – either he is trying to extricate himself from an entanglement with a girl he can't stand or he is trying to become permanently entangled with a girl he is mad about. (The girls he doesn't like are either too intellectual and stuffy or too flighty and 'soupy', and they have names like Madeline Bassett, Hermione Bostock, and Honoria Glossop. The girls he goes for are down-to-earth, spunky, and full of fun and disrespect, and they have names like Stiffy Byng, Bobbie Wickham, and Corky Pirbright.) Among the supporting types one frequently meets in Wodehouse are ponderous butlers, dim-witted clergymen, American millionaires with inflexible wills and incurable dyspepsia, incredibly vain literary lions, assorted crooks and gold-diggers, and Hollywood producers who go around signing up young English writers named Tennyson thinking they've snagged the poet.

It is always a bright spring morning or a soft summer evening in Wodehouseland. The action, though Wodehouse's plots are extremely Byzantine, usually revolves around nothing more earthshaking than the recovery of a stolen silver cow creamer or a prize Black Berkshire sow. The *Sturm und Drang* of the outside, or real, world hardly ever make an indentation. In the celebrated short story called 'The Clicking of Cuthbert' (1922), there are some allusions to Communist Russia (Vladimir Brusiloff, a visiting Russian novelist who turns out to be a golf fanatic, says to Cuthbert, 'Let me tell you one vairy funny story about putting. It was one day I play at Nijni-Novgorod with the pro against Lenin and Trotsky, and Trotsky has a two-inch putt for the hole. But, just as he addresses the ball, someone in the crowd he tries to assassinate Lenin with a rewolwer – you know that is our great national sport, trying to assassinate Lenin with rewolwers – and the bang puts Trotsky off his stroke and he goes five yards past the hole . . . and we win the hole and match and clean up three hundred and ninety-six thousand roubles, or fifteen shillings in your money'), and in the novel *The Code of the Woosters*, written after Oswald Mosley's Fascist Blackshirts had come to prominence in England, Roderick Spode, the 'heavy', is depicted as the leader of a new political force whose adherents wear black shorts, but it is hard to think of other instances in which Wodehouse leans on current events for his laughs.

In this general connection – the unrealness of Wodehouse's world – Richard Usborne, the English writer who is the ranking authority on Wodehouse, pointed out in his brilliant book *Wodehouse at Work* (1961), that despite the profusion of romances in the novels and short stories, only one sentence in one novel, *Jill the Reckless*, offers the slightest suggestion that 'a nice girl can be physically aroused'. (The sentence goes, 'The touch of his body against hers always gave her a thrill, half pleasurable, half exciting', and, at that, Jill is thinking only of cab rides.) When a Wodehouse hero and heroine first gaze into each others' eyes and recognize that they are in love, they are likely to head for a bedroom, but it is always the bedroom of someone they both loathe, and the purpose of their expedition is to 'apple-pie' that person's bed.

When you stand back and look at this never-never land, so innocent, sun-drenched, and quaint, it hardly seems the stuff that best-selling novels are made on. In Wodehouse's hands, it is. His narratives have thrust, his dialogue explodes, his characters come quickly and amusingly to life. In short, he possesses the uncommon gift of being able to tell a story that is great fun to read. The earlier writer he most closely resembles, perhaps, is Charles Dickens – the young Dickens of the *Pickwick Papers*, who created Samuel Pickwick, Sam Weller, and Alfred Jingle. Just as the *Pickwick Papers* is essentially a triumph of high spirits, so is the best of Wodehouse. To appreciate Wodehouse's art, one must, of course, read him at some length, but a few excerpts may serve to convey his special quality:

> I turned to the Right Hon. I even went so far as to pat him on the back. It was like slapping a wet sponge.
> 'All is well,' I said. 'Jeeves is coming.'
> 'What can he do?'
> I frowned a trifle. The man's tone had been peevish, and I didn't like it.
> 'That,' I replied with a touch of stiffness, 'we cannot say until

we see him in action. He may pursue one course, or he may pursue another. But on one thing you can rely with the utmost confidence – Jeeves will find a way. See, here he comes stealing through the undergrowth, his face shining with the light of pure intelligence. There are no limits to Jeeves' brain power. He virtually lives on fish.'

'But, dash it, we can't stop here,' said Pongo.

Lord Ickenham raised his eyebrows.

'Not stop here? Are you suggesting that we go out into that rain? My dear lad, you are not aware of the grave issues involved. This morning, as I was leaving home, I had a rather painful disagreement with your aunt. She said the weather was treacherous and wished me to take my woolly muffler. I replied that the weather was not treacherous and that I would be dashed if I took my woolly muffler. Eventually, by the exercise of an iron will, I had my way, and I ask you, my dear boy, to envisage what will happen if I return with a cold in my head. I shall sink to the level of a fifth-class power.'

He sang as he floated along, naturally selecting his favourite melody, and he had just got as far as the line about nests of robins in the hair and was rendering it with even more than his customary *brio* when there impinged upon his ears one of the gloomier passages of 'Old Man River', and he perceived coming towards him the bowed figure of the chap Weatherby.

When a man singing 'Trees' meets a man singing 'Old Man River' something has to give. They cannot both continue to function. Lord Holbeton generously decided to be the one to yield. It gave him a slight pang not to be able to do the high, wobbly note on the 'hair', but a man learns to take the rough with the smooth.

'Hello,' he said. 'What ho.'

Whereas Dickens' work became increasingly grim and gloomy as he grew older, Wodehouse never wrote a serious book or had the least desire to do so. Unlike most humorists, he was a basically cheerful man. 'Ziegfeld used to tell me that he wished he had my disposition,' he once told a friend who had commented on his sunniness. 'I seem to be rather good at adjusting to things. I think that must have something to do with it.' Then, too, as Wodehouse was well aware, life had been kind to him in many important ways. He had enjoyed almost uninterrupted good health. He had had an exceedingly happy marriage, to the former Ethel Newton Rowley, a crisp and energetic woman four years his junior, whom he met in the summer of 1914 and proposed to within a week. He had had a wonderful friend for over fifty years in Guy Bolton, the playwright, with whom he had worked on some twenty musical shows, Bolton writing the book and Wodehouse the lyrics. To top things off, Wodehouse had made a good bit of money, starting relatively early in his career, and this had enabled him to live in nice houses in pleasant places and to do pretty much what he wanted to. However, no one seems to get through life unscathed, and Wodehouse didn't. Indeed, during the Second World War he underwent one of the cruellest experiences that can befall a man: he was unjustly charged with being a traitor to his country. And his case demonstrates that people tend to remember a person's being accused of something dreadful much more vividly than they remember his eventually receiving a clean bill of health.

The whole tragic, complicated business began in the spring of 1940, when the German Army overran Belgium and northern France. Wodehouse was then living in the French resort town of Le Touquet, on the English Channel, with his wife and their usual houseful of dogs and cats. As an enemy alien, he was taken prisoner by the Germans, but for a couple of months this meant merely that he was confined to his house except on Saturday mornings, when he was required to report in person to the German *Kommandant* at Paris Plage, a few miles away.

In midsummer, there was a change. Wodehouse and

some fifty other male enemy aliens in that area were rounded up and, after varying periods in Loos Prison, Liège Barracks, and the Citadel of Huy, all in Belgium, were taken to Tost, in Upper Silesia. (Mrs Wodehouse, meanwhile, had gone to Hesdin, in northern France, hoping her husband would soon be released.) At Huy, there had been one stretch when the prisoners were so starved that they ate paper and matches, but at Tost, which was an internment camp and not a concentration camp, conditions were all right. Wodehouse soon resumed his old practice of starting off the morning with his daily dozen and then spending the bulk of the day writing. By the late winter of 1941, he had completed one novel, *Money in the Bank* – about an eccentric peer who puts all his money into diamonds and then mislays the lot – and had embarked on a second, a Blandings Castle story called *Full Moon*, which he expected to have wrapped up by October. In that month, he would become sixty, the age at which enemy aliens were supposed to be released. During this period, Wodehouse's friends had been busy on his behalf. A number of people in the United States, galvanized by Guy Bolton and his wife, Virginia, had got up an impressive petition and presented it to the German chargé d'affaires in Washington. The petition noted that Wodehouse had never been engaged in political or ideological activities, and it emphasized the fact that in a matter of months he would be sixty years old. It had some effect: Wodehouse was released from Tost in June 1941. He was told that he could take up residence in Berlin – where he would, of course, still be under house arrest – and he found space at the Adlon Hotel.

Wodehouse then made a terrible blunder. While he was at Tost, several correspondents from the American radio networks – the United States was still neutral – had asked him if he wanted to go on the air for them. He had not committed himself then, but at the Adlon, when he was again approached – this time by Harry Flannery, of the Columbia Broadcasting System – he was delighted to accept; he had received hundreds of solicitous letters at Tost and had not been able to answer them, and, as he saw it, there could hardly be a better way to assure his friends and fans of his well-being than by talking on the radio. This was the reason why he also accepted at this time an invitation from German radio officials to make a series of five broadcasts between 26 June and 2 July 1941 – broadcasts which he thought were intended solely to be sent by shortwave to the United States. He talked about Loos, Liège, Huy, and Tost, and he tried, in his usual way, to make light of his experiences – remarking, for instance, 'There is a good deal to be said for internment. It keeps you out of the pub and helps you to keep up with your reading.' Only a person as politically naïve and as fundamentally unworldly as Wodehouse would have failed to realize that the Nazi propaganda organization would record these talks, beam them to Britain, and generally exploit them for all they were worth. Wodehouse also failed to realize that in June 1941 Britain was fighting for its life, and that in those tense, desperate days anyone who broadcast on the German radio was considered *ipso facto* a collaborator – another Lord Haw-Haw. And certainly this was not the moment the British public wanted to hear Wodehouse or anyone else telling the world about how he had suffered no ill treatment at the hands of the Germans, or elaborating on a humanitarian credo ('Just as I am about to feel belligerent about some country, I meet a decent sort of chap. We go out together and lose any fighting thoughts or feelings'). After Alfred Duff Cooper, the Minister of Information, had given the cue, Wodehouse was flayed in the British press and on the radio as a traitor of the worst kind. It was falsely reported that he had made a deal with the Nazis to do the broadcasts in return for being released from the internment camp. As the outcry against him mounted, libraries threw out his books, and some clubs and associations he had belonged to struck his name from their lists.

Not until some three years later – in 1944, when the entire course of the war had changed and the Allies were well on their way to winning – did certain members of the British intelligentsia come to realize that the nation had panicked badly in its handling of the affair and had done Wodehouse a gross injustice. One of the first people to take Wodehouse's side was Muggeridge, who saw him in Paris (where Wodehouse had been allowed to go in 1943 and join his wife) at the time of the Liberation. In July of 1945, the first major article about the Wodehouse affair, Orwell's 'In Defence of P. G. Wodehouse', appeared in *Windmill* magazine. Between these two dates, in December 1944 the significant event had taken place. Anthony Eden, the Foreign Minister, was questioned in the House of Commons about whether the government intended to return Wodehouse to England and bring him to trial for high treason, and in his reply he exonerated Wodehouse completely. The matter had been thoroughly gone into, Eden said, and there was 'no question of a trial, and no question of a charge'.

After the war, Wodehouse never returned to England. When he left Paris in 1947, he came to the United States, and he lived in New York City until the mid-1950s, when he moved out to Remsenburg. In 1956, he became an American citizen, as did Mrs Wodehouse, though both also retained their British citizenship. Some of Wodehouse's friends believe that the reason he chose not to return to England, even for a short visit, was a lingering bitterness not just over the unfair way he was treated but over even being considered the kind of man who would defect to the enemy – an attitude best summed up, per-haps, in a remark he made to his American literary agent, Scott Meredith: 'I may be a fool, but I am not a renegade.' However, in 1961, on the eve of his eightieth-birthday, Wodehouse's colleagues in Britain took the occasion to pay him, in the words of Evelyn Waugh, 'homage and reparation', and this was a source of deep gratification to him. Then, in 1965, the British Broadcasting Corporation, which had paid him a wonderful eightieth birthday trib-ute on the air, presented a television series about the adventures of Bertie Wooster and Jeeves. This proved to be so popular that two other series, one built around Lord Emsworth and the other around Ukridge, were also pro-duced. Though Wodehouse never actually put it in words, the people closest to him thought that they detected a definite change of heart in him as he moved into his late eighties, and they felt that he would have liked nothing better than to visit England again. 'Today, what with these 747s, transatlantic travel is no trouble at all,' Bolton observed. 'I must be sure to mention that to Wodehouse on one of our walks. I'd love to see him go back for his ninetieth birthday.'

—≡ 2 ≡—

Wodehouse was born in Guildford, Surrey, on 15 October 1881, the third of four sons of Henry Ernest Wodehouse, a Hong Kong magistrate, and Eleanor Deane Wodehouse, daughter of a clergyman from the Bath area. Mrs Wodehouse believed in giving her children imposing names. The eldest she called Philip Peveril John – Peveril because he was the first white child born on the Peak in Hong Kong and this brought to her mind Sir Walter Scott's *Peveril of the Peak*. The second she called Ernest Armine, Armine being a family name that the Wodehouses had used for centuries. 'Wodehouse', by the way, is pronounced as if it were spelled 'Woodhouse'. This orthographic peculiarity was a source of family pride, for it denoted membership in the Norfolk branch of the family – the branch headed by the Earl of Kimberley. (*Burke's Peerage* notes, 'The name of Wodehouse first occurs in Norfolk in 1402 when John Wodehouse was made Constable of Castle Rising.')

Mrs Wodehouse named her third son Pelham Grenville after his godfather, Colonel Pelham Grenville Von Donop, who was a prominent member of the English colony in Hong Kong. Her fourth son she named Richard Lancelot Deane. From the start, Pelham was called Plum by the family. 'If you say Pelham quickly, it comes out sounding something like Plum,' Wodehouse explained. 'I rather liked it, particularly after I learned, during my boyhood, that a famous Middlesex cricketer, Pelham Warner, was called Plum. He captained England a number of times.'

The Wodehouse boys, like the children of many British civil servants and military men scattered around the globe, had a minimum of home life. Pelham, for example, after spending his infancy in Hong Kong, returned to England with the family in 1885, when his father's leave came round, as it did every fourth year. The following year, when his parents went back to the Far East, Pelham was deposited with a family in Croydon that also looked after his older brothers. At eight, he was sent to a boarding school on the island of Guernsey, and after two years there he was transferred to a boarding school in Dover. In the summer of 1894, he entered Dulwich College and he stayed there for six years, until he was approaching nineteen. If his parents happened to be in England, he spent his school holidays with them. Otherwise, he was passed around among his relatives.

'I suppose I had the same kind of boyhood Kipling had,' Wodehouse once remarked, 'The difference was that he hated his but I found mine very pleasant.' One of the main reasons was that, by and large, Wodehouse enjoyed his time away from school very much. He especially liked his visits to Ham Hill, near Worcester, the estate of his paternal grandmother; a Birmingham heiress, she had married Colonel Philip Wodehouse, a veteran of the battle of Waterloo. Young Pelham also found two of his maternal aunts exceedingly agreeable – Aunt Julie, who lived in Bath and had three beautiful daughters, and Aunt Emmaline (or Nim), a portrait painter and an amusing talker, who had a house in Cheyne Walk, Chelsea. Aunt Emmaline was a spinster, and so were three other sisters – Aunt Mary, Aunt Louisa (or Loulie), and Aunt Anne, who lived together in Cheney Court, an elegant country house at Box, near Bath. On his father's side of the family, too, there were lots of relatives to visit: Aunt Lydia, a spinster who had a little flat in London; Aunt Edith and Uncle Gussie, who lived in Dover; Aunt Constance and Uncle Philip, who was the rector of Bratton Fleming, in Devonshire; Aunt Alice and Uncle Fred, who was the rector of Gotham, in Nottinghamshire; Aunt Jane and Uncle William; and Aunt Amy and Uncle Albert. Is it any wonder there is such a high incidence of aunts and uncles in Wodehouse's stories?

It was also during this period of his life that Wodehouse became acquainted with the backstairs personnel who were to figure so prominently in his stories. His aunts and uncles used to take him along with them when they paid their calls at the local great houses, and he later wrote, 'Even at the age of ten, I was a social bust, contributing little or nothing to the feast of reason and flow of soul. The thing generally ended in my hostess smiling one of those painful smiles and suggesting it would be nice for your little nephew to go and have tea in the Servants' Hall. And she was right. I loved it. My mind today is fragrant with memories of kindly footmen and vivacious parlourmaids. In their society, I forgot to be shy and kidded back and forth with the best of them. And then . . . in would come the butler. . . . "The young gentleman is wanted," he would say morosely, and the young gentleman would shamble out.'

The chief reason Wodehouse's boyhood was a happy one, however, was Dulwich College. As the third son, he had been slated for the Royal Naval College at Dartmouth and a career in the Navy, but Armine was at Dulwich, and when Pelham went to visit his brother at school he fell in love with the place, and persuaded his father to let him go there. Dulwich, which is six miles south of London, was founded in 1619 by Edward Alleyn, who had been a leading actor in the Elizabethan theatre and then, under King James I, a master of the king's games. Though never as socially important or as influential as Eton, Harrow, or Winchester, Dulwich is regarded as a fine school. It is certainly a handsome one. Its principal buildings, North Italian Renaissance in style, are the work of Charles Barry, the son of the nineteenth-century architect who designed the Houses of Parliament, and they stand in a wide expanse of beautiful green parkland. Few urban schools have playing fields to compare with Dulwich's, and, partly for this reason, its rugby and cricket teams have been outstanding down through the years. In addition to a great many first-class athletes, Dulwich has produced a sizable number of graduates who gained fame in other pursuits – Ernest Shackleton, C. S. Forester, A. E. W. Mason, Leslie Howard, Hartley Shawcross, G. E. Moor, and Raymond Chandler, to name a few. (Chandler, an American, was brought up by an Irish uncle, who sent him to Dulwich because it was relatively inexpensive.)

In Wodehouse's time, there were six hundred boys at the school, most of them day students, so winning a place in an athletic team or excelling in any other way took some doing. Wodehouse did extremely well along a broad front. He was an editor of the school magazine, *The Alleynian.* His last two years, he was in both the rugby team and the cricket team. Being a good-sized young man – he stood a little over six feet and weighed about a hundred and eighty – he was a forward in rugby. In cricket, he was a fast bowler, and had his best day when he took seven wickets for forty runs against Tonbridge. He also did impressively well in his studies, and, as befitted a young man who actually enjoyed both Latin and Greek composition, he was one of four Senior Scholars in his class. (Two others were William Phelps, who became the

Assistant Assayer of the Royal Mint, and J. T. Sheppard, who attained considerable celebrity both as a classical scholar and as the flamboyant Provost of King's College, Cambridge.) Wodehouse's brother Armine had gone on from Dulwich to Oxford (where he was to win the Chancellor's Essay Prize and the Newdigate Poetry Prize), and Wodehouse planned to follow. He never got there. His father, who had to retire early because of poor health, simply didn't have the money to send him. 'His pension, for some reason or other, was pegged to the Indian rupee,' Wodehouse used to explain. 'The rupee was forever fluctuating, and in 1900 it went *phut*. That was all there was to it. I had to go out and get a job.'

It is hard to tell whether or not Wodehouse's affection for his public school would have been quite as strong had he gone on to the university, but in any case Dulwich remained extraordinarily close to his heart. When he was a mooringless young writer in London, he went back nearly every weekend to play or to watch sports and to visit old friends. Long after he had become successful – in fact, right up to the Second World War – he continued occasionally to write up the school cricket and rugby matches for *The Alleynian*. He was always a bundle of nerves at a crucial game. One year when the rugby team needed to win only the last match on its schedule to complete an undefeated season, Wodehouse, as was his custom, walked the six miles from London to Dulwich for the game. He was watching the action from the sidelines when he found the tension unbearable and quickly made his way outside the school gate and positioned himself at a spot where he could just hear the cries from the field and make out from them how the game was progressing. After the final whistle sounded a dramatic victory for Dulwich, he headed back to London on foot, but by that time his nerves were so utterly frazzled that later, when he tried to reconstruct the return journey in his mind, he couldn't remember a thing about it.

Wodehouse had no trouble finding a job in London. Through his father's connections, he became a member of what we would today call the training squad at the Hong Kong & Shanghai Bank, on Lombard Street. 'The idea was that a chap would put in two years or so learning the various aspects of the business,' Wodehouse recalls. 'Then he received his orders and went out as an under manager to Surabaja or some place like that.' Thanks to his ability to adjust to most situations, Wodehouse got to like the world of banking fairly well, but the prospect of spending his life in the Far East appalled him. The obvious solution was to find some other means of supporting himself, and to this end he turned to writing, which he had always liked. He wrote at night and on weekends. (Only one member of his family, his Aunt Mary – the aunt he liked least, and who was to serve as the model for Bertie Wooster's bossy, beaky Aunt Agatha – had done any professional writing. Not that anyone confused her with Jane Austen, but she was a novelist.) From the start, Wodehouse fared quite well. He sold light verse to the *Daily Chronicle*, and he sold short stories and humorous articles to periodicals like *Today*, *Answers*, *Tit Bits*, and the *Universal & Ludgate Magazine*. The usual payment was ten shillings for a poem and a pound or so for a story or an article. The break he needed in order to resign his bank job came in 1901, when William Beach Thomas, a young master at Dulwich who had given up teaching for journalism, arranged for Wodehouse to be his back-up man on the *Globe*, a London evening newspaper. Beach Thomas's job was that of assistant to Harold Begbie, an author of tearjerking novels who edited a daily front-page column called 'By the Way' – a potpourri of witty remarks, light verse, and sparkling comments on the news, which were supplied in part by the conductors of the column and in part by its readers. A year or two later, when Beach Thomas took off for greener fields (he was to become a famous war correspondent during the First World War and was knighted), Wodehouse succeeded him as Begbie's assistant. In his job, he was paid three pounds a week, which was an excellent income for a young man in London at that time. For example, Wodehouse's bed-sitting room in Walpole Street, Chelsea, cost him only twenty-one shillings a week, breakfast and dinner included.

In 1902, Wodehouse's first book, *The Pothunters*, was published. This was a story for boys, about public-school life, which had previously been serialized in the *Public School Magazine*. Around this time, too, he broke into the big time: he sold a set of verses to *Punch*, and he sold a short story about an Oxford-Cambridge rugby match to the *Strand*. (The editors of the *Strand* then decided that no one was interested in rugby, and changed it into a story about an Oxford–Cambridge soccer match.) In 1904, when Begbie left the *Globe*, Wodehouse took over as the editor of 'By the Way', at a salary of five pounds a week. He felt rich enough then to treat himself to a vacation trip to the United States.

Wodehouse spent almost the whole of his visit in New York City, but made one foray into Westchester to interview Kid McCoy, who was training in White Plains for his bout with Philadelphia Jack O'Brien for the world welterweight championship. 'After that trip to New York, I was someone who counted', he wrote many years later. 'The manner of editors changed towards me. Where before it had been "Throw this man out," they now said "Come in, my dear fellow, come in and tell us all about America." When some intricate aspect of American politics had to be explained to the British public, it was "Ask

Wodehouse. Wodehouse will know." My income rose like a rocketing pheasant. I made £505.1.7 in 1906 and £527.17.1 in 1907 and was living, I suppose, on about £203.4.9. In fact, if, on November 17, 1907, had I not bought a secondhand Darracq car for £450 (and smashed it up in the first week) I should soon have been one of those economic royalists who get themselves so disliked. This unfortunate venture brought my capital back to where it had started, and a long and dusty road had to be travelled before my finances were in a state sufficiently sound to justify another visit to the land of my dreams.'

Wodehouse made that second visit to the States in 1909. Between the two trips, he continued to run 'By the Way', but this took up only his mornings, so he had ample time to pursue various freelance projects. Among the new jobs he took on, the one that interested him most was that of resident encore lyricist at the Aldwych Theatre. (Later, he held the same post at the Gaiety as well.) What it meant was this: After a musical comedy had settled down for a long run, if it happened to contain a hit song, or songs, featuring catchy patter lyrics in the style of W. S. Gilbert, there would inevitably come a time when the encore lyricist would have to provide fresh sets of lyrics, so that the stars could continue to titillate the audience when they were called back for encore chorus after encore chorus. Occasionally, Wodehouse was given a chance to write the lyrics for whole songs in Aldwych and Gaiety musicals. His big opportunity came in 'The Beauty of Bath', the London show for which Jerome Kern wrote the show-stopper, a song called 'Mr Chamberlain' in which Wodehouse demonstrated unusual dexterity in devising lyrics that detailed with just the right humorous twist the main points of Joseph Chamberlain's protective tariff policy.

He also continued to pound out novels about public-school life, at the rate of one a year. Only one of these is worth mentioning – *Mike*, which was first published in 1909 and most recently republished (1953) in two volumes: *Mike at Wrykyn* and *Mike and Psmith*. George Orwell called *Mike* one of the best 'light' school stories in the English language, and countless Old Boys have shared this opinion, but it is an important book on another ground as well, for it marked the occasion in Wodehouse's career when he was able to shift into high gear and reveal himself as a writer of exceptional comic powers. He achieved this by creating his first major character, Psmith. A reedy, monocled, wealthy young man of eighteen, Psmith is a non-stop talker, but he is well worth listening to, because he has a vivid way of expressing himself and, furthermore, seems to know the ways of the world better than most men three times his age. He is a poor student, though, and when we meet him in *Mike* his father has just yanked him out of Eton and sent him to Sedleigh, an unglamorous, rather ordinary school that has a reputation for making good students out of balky material. At Sedleigh, he becomes close friends with Mike Jackson, a transfer from Wrykyn, a fictional public school that is the setting for a number of Wodehouse's early stories. Mike is a prodigy at cricket, and his father has sent him to Sedleigh, where there is little emphasis on that game, in the hope that he will be able to get down to his studies there. The second half of *Mike* describes how Mike and Psmith, who have no intention of taking Sedleigh seriously during the short time they must spend there before moving on, presumably to Cambridge, gradually undergo a change of heart and become rather devoted to their new school. Mike arranges a cricket match with Wrykyn, which Sedleigh wins, largely because of his own sensational performance, and this is a significant victory: it means that in the years ahead Sedleigh will be able to schedule cricket matches with much better schools than in the past.

In a follow-up novel, *Psmith in the City*, published in 1910, Psmith and Mike are reunited in London. Unlike most novelists, Wodehouse rarely makes use of autobiographical material, but he does so in *Psmith in the City*. We learn at the start of the story that Mike's father has suffered severe financial reverses, and Mike, instead of entering Cambridge, must go to work in a bank in London – the New Asiatic Bank, as a matter of fact. He hates every moment of it, but life becomes a good deal more palatable when Psmith, of all people, joins the staff. The climax of the story arrives when Mike receives an urgent phone call one morning from his older brother Joe, the captain of their county cricket team, asking him if he can come up to Lord's immediately and fill in in a big match against Middlesex. It seems there has been an auto accident and the team is short a man. Mike is well aware that he will lose his job at the bank if he takes time off to play in the match, but he decides to do so anyway. He is in top form, and scores a dazzling century. Everything turns out happily in the end. Psmith, a talented operator, fixes things so that his own father, who is mad about cricket, will pay Mike's way through Cambridge, after which Mike will become the estate manager of the senior Psmith's country place. Fair enough.

Psmith made two return appearances – in *Psmith Journalist*, published in 1915, and *Leave It to Psmith*, published in 1923. The surprising thing is that there weren't more Psmith books, for Wodehouse was very fond of Psmith and enjoyed writing about him. 'I think the reason Psmith came off so well was that he was based on a real person,' he said not long ago. 'He was modelled on a boy named Rupert D'Oyly Carte – the son of the Gilbert and Sullivan man – who was at Winchester with a cousin of mine, Jim

Deane. Jim was fascinated by him and loved telling us about him. I never did get to meet young D'Oyly Carte. Of course, that could be the best way to get a chap – to hear all about him but not to know him personally. Then you're likely to be too close.' Be that as it may, Psmith emerged as the first in the long line of extraordinary talkers one encounters in Wodehouse. Straight talk bores Psmith. He rarely refers to tea as tea; it is 'a cup of the steaming'. For Psmith, people never end up in the soup; no, they land 'with a splash in the very centre of the Oxo'. And so on.

According to Richard Usborne, the fondness that Psmith and other Wodehouse characters show for the substitute phrase – the more orotund the better – derives principally from the verbal style of the Knut, the slang Edwardian term for the good-natured, abstracted fop. By way of illustration, Usborne pointed out that Lord Tidmouth, a Knutty character in a 1927 play called *Good Morning, Bill*, adapted by Wodehouse from a Hungarian play, used half a dozen different substitutes for 'goodbye': 'bung-ho,' 'teuf-teuf,' 'toodle-oo,' 'tinkerty-tonk', 'poo-boop-a-doop', and 'honk-honk'. This is the start of an astute and entertaining exercise in literary genealogy in which Usborne tries to trace the ancestors of Wodehouse's style. The formal, recitative manner employed by Psmith, and later by such talented raconteurs as Lord Ickenham and Galahad Threepwood, is an echo, Usborne believes, of Arthur Conan Doyle's narrative voice in his Sherlock Holmes stories. Closely allied with this is the parody use by Psmith – and later by Jeeves, somewhat differently – of the stilted language of 'First Leaders, school sermons, toastmasters, and treaties'. The 'absurdly inflated phrases' and 'false concords' that form such an appealing part of the speech of Bertie Wooster and other talented Wodehouse fumblers show, according to Usborne, the influence of F. Anstey's *Baboo Jabberjee*, a near-classic, published in 1897, in which Hurry Bungsho Jabberjee, an over-earnest law student from India, recounts his experiences in England. Finally there is the device whereby Psmith and other Wodehouse characters, without crediting the source or changing their tone of voice, slip from their own words into some well-known poem and then, after rattling off a number of lines, segue smoothly back into their own stuff – a routine pioneered by Dickens, via Dick Swiveller, in *The Old Curiosity Shop*.

Wodehouse found these observations of Usborne's very interesting. 'When I was a schoolboy and a young man, Conan Doyle and Dickens were indeed two of my favourite authors, and I admired Anstey highly,' he remarked to a friend. 'If reading them had any especial effect on my manner of writing, I must say I was never aware of it. Of course, one never knows those things. I would guess that Barry Pain had as much influence on my writing as anyone. No one, I gather, reads Barry Pain today, but he was awfully good. He wrote for magazines like *Pearson's* – fifteen-hundred-word humorous sketches about, say, a waiter or a jabbering gardener. He was marvellous at creating a character in a few swift strokes. I have all of his books.'

$$=3=$$

Wodehouse's second visit to the United States substantially changed the course of his life. He was intending to stay only a few weeks, but shortly after he arrived in New York he sold two short stories he had brought over with him – one to *Collier's*, for three hundred dollars, and the other to *Cosmopolitan*, for two hundred dollars. In England, the top price he had ever received for a short story was ten pounds and, his ears still ringing with the buoying assurance that both *Cosmopolitan* and *Collier's* wanted to see more of his work, he sent the *Globe* a letter of resignation and moved into the Earle Hotel, on Waverly Place. It probably comes as a shock to most Wodehouse fans to learn that he has spent by far the greater part of his adult life in America. The picture of Wodehouse that his readers invariably conjure up has him ambling across a crisp sward in Sussex or Shropshire, swinging a knobbly walking stick and humming 'Roses of Picardy'. They find it almost impossible to picture him living in a room in Greenwich Village or, as he did many years later, in a penthouse apartment on Park Avenue.

As it turned out, Wodehouse was unable to sell another short story to either *Collier's* or *Cosmopolitan*. For the next four years, he kept himself afloat by grinding out stories and articles for *Munsey's*, *Popular*, *McClure's*, *Ainslee's*, *Argosy*, and other pulp magazines. Then, in 1914, things began to break for him. To begin with, the *Saturday Evening Post* bought the serialization rights to a novel he had just finished, *Something Fresh*, for thirty-five hundred dollars – a stupendous sum in those days. George Horace Lorimer, who was then editing the *Post*, also told Wodehouse he wanted to see more of his work, but this time the results were happier. The following year, Lorimer bought the rights to Wodehouse's next novel, *Uneasy Money*, and this time paid him five thousand dollars. Wodehouse and the *Post* continued to do business together for decades. All in all, the *Post* serialized no fewer than twenty-one of his novels and steadily increased his payments until in 1938 he reached a top of forty-five thousand dollars for *Summer Moonshine*.

In 1969, in a preface that Wodehouse supplied for a new British edition of *Something Fresh* (in America it is called *Something New*), he noted, in a typical flight of fancy, that what had probably put Lorimer in such a receptive mood towards the original manuscript back in 1914 was that on the title page he had departed from his usual practice of calling himself P. G. Wodehouse and, for the first time, cut loose with the full blast – Pelham Grenville Wodehouse. 'A writer in America at that time who went about without three names was practically going around naked,' he explained. 'Those were the days of Richard Harding Davis, James Warner Bellah, Margaret Culkin Banning, Earl Derr Biggers, Charles Francis Coe, Norman Reilly Raine, Mary Roberts Rinehart, Clarence Budington Kelland, and Orison Swett – yes, really, I'm not kidding – Marden. Naturally, a level-headed editor like Lorimer was not going to let a Pelham Grenville Wodehouse get away from him.'

What had really happened – as no one realized more clearly than Wodehouse himself – was that he had hit upon the kind of story about England and Englishmen that Americans went for. The readers of the *Post*, who had just fallen in love with *Ruggles of Red Gap*, were delighted to meet up, in *Something Fresh*, with another English butler, the formidable Beach, who went about his duties with 'dignified inertia' and spoke in a voice 'like old tawny port made audible'. *Something Fresh* also contained a number of other ingredients that were to work well for Wodehouse. It was the first of his novels to be set in a sprawling country house – in this instance, Blandings Castle. It served to introduce Lord Emsworth, who proved to be one of his most durable characters. And it introduced Lord Emsworth's younger son, the Honourable Freddie Threepwood, who was the first of Wodehouse's doltish young 'dudes' – a genus that was to reach its full flowering in Bertie Wooster. It is instructive to note that *Uneasy Money*, the second novel that Wodehouse sold to the *Post*, also contained a butler, a large country house, and a dudish young hero. It should be pointed out that both novels had one other thing going for them: they were exceedingly well written. Wodehouse had found his vein of humour and had arrived at the tone and style that soon became synonymous with his name, as the superb opening paragraphs of *Uneasy Money* show:

In a day in June, at the hour when London moves abroad in quest of lunch, a young man stood at the entrance of the Bandolero Restaurant looking earnestly up Shaftesbury Avenue – a large young man in excellent condition, with a pleasant, good-humoured, brown, clean-cut face. He paid no attention to the stream of humanity that flowed past him. His mouth was set and his eyes wore a serious, almost wistful expression. He was frowning slightly. One would have said that here was a man with a secret sorrow.

William FitzWilliam Delamere Chalmers, Lord Dawlish, had no secret sorrow. All that he was thinking of at that moment was the best method of laying a golf ball dead in front of the

Palace Theatre. It was his habit to pass the time in mental golf when Claire Fenwick was late in keeping her appointments with him. On one occasion she had kept him waiting so long that he had been able to do nine holes, starting at the Savoy Grill and finishing up near Hammersmith. His was a simple mind, able to amuse itself with simple things.

At about this time, Wodehouse's private life also took a decided turn upward. When he was halfway through *Something Fresh*, Norman Thwaites, an English friend on the staff of the New York *World*, introduced him to a pretty young widow named Ethel Rowley, who had come over here from England on a visit. Wodehouse was smitten with her instantly and totally – much in the fashion later made famous by such hypervulnerable members of the Drones Club as Bingo Little and Freddie Widgeon. The following Sunday, he took Mrs Rowley out to see his favourite seaside spot – Bellport, on the South Shore of Long Island. On the train trip back to New York, their relationship reached a critical juncture. As they were chatting cozily, Wodehouse was seized with a fit of sneezing, and after it had continued for a while Mrs Rowley suggested that it might be better all around if he took an empty seat across the aisle. He did so, reluctantly. The next half hour, feeling increasingly miserable in his exile, he sat watching her as she unconcernedly read her newspaper. Then he could stand the separation no longer. He got up, proposed to her, and was accepted. They were married on 30 September 1914, in the Little Church Around the Corner. 'I remember our wedding very clearly,' Wodehouse said many years later. 'We were standing around inside the church waiting for the minister when this young chap came bounding in. "I've just made ten thousand dollars in the stock market," he announced. This was the minister, naturally.'

At the time of his marriage, Wodehouse was two weeks

away from his thirty-third birthday. He was a tall, husky, good-looking fellow with dark-brown hair and a square jaw. He wore glasses, and had since his teens, because he was extremely nearsighted. (Because of his defective eyesight, he was refused for military service during the First World War.) As a boy, he had been on the shy side – 'I was rather unsophisticated and not good at conversation' is the way he puts it – and though some of the shyness had now rubbed away, he still avoided large, glittering parties whenever he could. He did not say flashingly witty things – he was in no way a performer – but in his talk there was a good deal of humour, particularly for a humorist. Above all, he was gentle and unfailingly considerate. Apart from this, his outstanding trait was his industry. He was an indefatigable worker. In addition to writing his novels and short stories, he started at this time to contribute regularly to *Vanity Fair*, whipping up, at the request of Frank Crowninshield, who had recently become its editor, frothy pieces on subjects like the income tax and the present state of the East Coast débutante. He was soon turning these pieces out at such a rate that, at Crowninshield's suggestion, he took to using pseudonyms, so that the magazine wouldn't look to be too much the work of one man. Although he had now decided that his permanent literary signature would be P. G. Wodehouse, for *Vanity Fair* he also became J. Plum, Pelham Grenville, P. Brook-Haven (after the Long Island town near Bellport), C. P. West (for Central Park West), and J. Walker Williams (from the vaudeville team of Walker and Williams).

In 1915, Wodehouse became *Vanity Fair's* drama critic, and in that capacity, on Christmas night, he attended the opening performance at the Princess Theatre of *Very Good, Eddie*, a musical comedy for which Guy Bolton had written the book and Jerome Kern the music. After the show, he went backstage to see Kern, whom he had worked with in London, and Kern introduced him to Bolton, a young transatlantic type – a member of a famous old family of Savannah cotton-shippers – who, after being born and brought up in England, had been sent to military school in Nyack, and was studying architecture in an atelier in New York City when he blossomed out as a successful playwright, with a comedy about divorce called *The Rule of Three*. That Christmas night, Wodehouse accompanied Kern and Bolton to Kern's apartment, where they went to sweat out the reviews in the morning papers. 'The notices were fine,' Bolton recalled a few years ago. 'But the big thing that happened that night – or morning – was that Kern and I invited Wodehouse to join us in our next show. We needed a lyricist, and Kern, who knew Wodehouse's work, was sure he was just the man. What we were aiming at in our shows was charm and taste. That was what you had to aim at if you were working at the Princess, because it was such a small theatre. It stood on Sixth Avenue at Thirty-ninth Street, under the "L", and I think it had only two hundred and ninety-nine seats. The stage was too small for a full chorus line, and, if I remember correctly, the pit could accommodate only twelve musicians. In a way, these limitations were an advantage: the "Princess shows", as they were called, were the first intimate musical comedies. That was the quality we strove to get in our shows wherever they were playing, and once Wodehouse was back in the theatre, writing those delightful lyrics of his, we were well on the way to achieving our object.'

Kern, Bolton, and Wodehouse did two Princess shows – *Oh, Boy!* and *Oh, Lady! Lady!!* – and a half-dozen other superior musicals, ending with *Sitting Pretty* in 1924. In addition, at times when Bolton was committed to other projects, Wodehouse did a few shows with Kern for which someone else provided the book. Similarly, when Bolton, after several false starts, succeeding in putting together the show that became *Sally*, all the music was by Kern, but Wodehouse was just one of several lyricists involved. Wodehouse also provided lyrics for a number of other composers who wrote for the theatre, among them Rudolf Friml, Emmerich Kalman, Felix (Ivan) Caryll, Ivor Novello, and George Gershwin, but he was unquestionably most at home working in troika with Kern and Bolton, and it is not surprising that the three big hit songs with which he was associated were all written for their shows – 'The Siren's Song', for *Leave It to Jane*; 'Till The Clouds Roll By,' for *Oh, Boy!*; and 'Bill', for *Oh, Lady! Lady!!* Midway through the rehearsals of *Oh, Lady! Lady!!* 'Bill' was dropped from the show – it wasn't suited to the voice of the leading lady, Vivienne Segal – and it remained unsung and unknown for nine years, until Kern, working on *Show Boat* and needing a strong ballad for Helen Morgan, happened to remember it. (More than one successful cadger of drinks has based his career on betting popular-music buffs that they couldn't name the man who wrote the words for 'Bill'.)

Wodehouse loved writing lyrics and looked upon it as a form of recreation, but, for all that, doing a Broadway show took time and trouble for men whose standards were high. 'Wodehouse and I worked together very closely,' Bolton has said. 'Most people have somehow picked up the idea that integrating the story and lyrics of a musical comedy began with *Oklahoma!* I don't know how that notion got started, for I can assure you that Wodehouse, Kern, and I made a conscious effort to fuse all the elements of our shows. It was my job to write the book, but I always discussed the story line and the characters in great detail with Wodehouse and got his ideas. Then, when things were beginning to take shape, we'd decide where, say, to stop the dialogue and put the end of a scene into a lyric – things like that. When I finished the first draft of a scene, or a series of scenes, I'd send it round to Wodehouse with a note telling him that if he saw something that could be improved he should go ahead and tickle it up. Quite often, at this stage of the game, we might revise our first thoughts about the placement of a song, or even the kind of song it should be. It was a very careful collaboration, and a most congenial one.'

In those days, the composer customarily received three per cent of the show's net receipts, the writer of the book two per cent, and the lyricist one per cent. It was Wodehouse's and Bolton's practice to take one and a half per cent each, and Wodehouse would recompense Bolton for the extra half per cent by giving him fifty per cent of the royalties from the songs. Wodehouse also enjoyed an unusually amicable relationship with Kern. The composer and his lyricist worked two ways – sometimes Wodehouse wrote the words to fit Kern's music, and sometimes Kern wrote the music to fit Wodehouse's words. As a rule, if it was an upbeat or comedy song the lyric came first, and if it was a romantic or reflective song the music did. 'Everyone remembers Jerry Kern for his lovely melodies, but his talent went far beyond that,' Wodehouse told a young composer. 'People have no idea what a skilful showman he was. Jerry could set *anything* you wrote to music, easily and effectively.'

Wodehouse, for his part, was an almost ideal lyricist. He had fun in the patter songs he wrote for trios and duets, but he never forced a funny or tricky rhyme if he thought it would interfere with the sense of the lyric or with the motion of the music. He liked the lift that an internal rhyme gave, but he preferred such a rhyme to be unobtrusive, as it is in that well-known line from 'Bill': 'are not the kind that you would find in a statue'. He was adept at fitting his words to Kern's music, and felt that this approach led to some of his best work. 'If a lyric writer does the words first, he has a tendency to fall into certain set metrical patterns. I know that I found it very stimulating when Jerry did the melody first and went sailing off in some new direction. Then I *had* to follow. Another reason I think you frequently end up with a good lyric when the music is written first is that you know where the high spots of the melody come, and you try to match the high spots of your lyrics to them.' Wodehouse's certificate of membership in the American Society of Composers, Authors, and Publishers hung on the wall of his study, beside an official notice from Oxford University that it planned to bestow on him an honorary doctorate in literature.

It was during this period, when everything was breaking his way, that Wodehouse's books – and they are what one thinks of first when one thinks of Wodehouse – finally began to sell in large quantities, both in America and in Britain. In 1917, in what proved to be a wise move, he decided to change over to a new British publisher, Herbert Jenkins. Jenkins had started out as a writer of broad, middle-class humour – most of it in stories that revolved around a Cockney character named Bindle – but he had quickly made a reputation as an acute and progressive businessman. One of several new ideas he had come up with to stimulate sales, which apparently it did, was to print a synopsis of the plot of a novel ('What This Story Is About') on its dust jacket. In any event, the average sale of a Wodehouse book had previously hovered around two thousand copies, but *Piccadilly Jim*, the first book of his that Jenkins published, sold more than nine thousand. Jenkins' forte, however, was the cheap edition, and when *Piccadilly Jim* came out as a half-crown reprint, in 1920, it sold an incredible two hundred thousand copies. *A*

Damsel in Distress, the second Wodehouse novel published by Jenkins, fared almost as sensationally. Wodehouse's subsequent books did not do quite so well, but by this time the hard-cover edition of each new novel or collection of short stories invariably galloped through a number of printings before slowing down. Then the work would be brought out in a cheaper hard-cover edition or in paper-back. Jenkins died in the early 1920s, but the firm bore his name for many years before it was merged into a company called Barrie and Jenkins, which is now part of the Hutchinson Publishing Group. Down through the years, he was the company's only high-powered author, and his books were its biggest sellers, although it had had a very good thing in an encyclopedia called *Enquire Within upon Everything*, which told you how to get stains out of garments, how to plant musk roses, and so on. The firm always prized Wodehouse, but nothing it ever did for him pleased him more than its inauguration, a dozen years ago, of the medium-priced Autograph Edition of his books.

Wodehouse got around to one more thing during his magnificent burst of achievement in the second half of the century's second decade: he invented his two most popular characters – Bertie Wooster, the ultimate English upper-class innocent, and Jeeves, the scholarly and resourceful valet. For a team that is now spoken of in the same breath as Don Quixote and Sancho Panza or Samuel Pickwick and Sam Weller when the great master-and-servant partnerships of literature are discussed, Wooster and Jeeves got off slowly. When Jeeves made his début, in a 1916 short story called 'Extricating Young Gussie', he had only three lines of dialogue: 'Mrs Gregson to see you, sir,' and, later, 'Very good, sir. Which suit will you wear?' For that matter, Bertie had not yet emerged whole and distinct, either. The protagonist in 'Extricating

Young Gussie' is called Bertie, all right, but he bears the stagy last name of Mannering-Phipps. In the next four short stories in which Jeeves figures, Wodehouse renamed his Bertie character Reggie Pepper. After this, he became Bertie again and took on the less fluttery family name of Wooster.

It was in a short story called 'The Artistic Career of Corky' that Wodehouse finally straightened out Bertie's relationship with Jeeves. Wodehouse explained it many years later by saying, 'Nobody has ever called Bertram Wooster one of our brightest minds; his friend Corky had even less of what it takes to solve life's difficulties, and they were faced by a major problem. Being a conscientious artist, I simply could not let either of them have a brilliant idea for solving, and yet someone had to have one or the story could not be written. In the upshot, the chap who had the brilliant idea was me. "Why not groom this bit player Jeeves for stardom?" I said to myself. "Why not," I said, still soliloquizing, "make him a bird with a terrific brain who comes to Bertie's rescue whenever the latter gets into a jam?" "Eureka," I would have cried only I did not want to steal Archimedes' stuff, and I got down to it without delay.'

═4═

Wodehouse, unlike a number of his colleagues who were similarly successful in the twenties, had no desire to run with the international set, and he continued to lead a restrained, orderly life. As usual, his closest friends were old friends. More often than not, they were people with whom he was associated in the theatre: in London, George Grossmith, a polished light comedian who became a successful producer, and Ian Hay, a fine playwright; in London and New York, Guy Bolton. It was a quiet life, but a very good one. In the 1920s and 1930s, Wodehouse spent some time each year in both London and New York, his transatlantic schedule being geared to the musical shows or plays he was involved in. He found that France offered him a nice change of pace, and on two occasions he was lured to Hollywood. In the late twenties and early thirties, when he put in his first stint – he worked on *Three French Girls* and *Rosalie* for Metro-Goldwyn-Mayer – he and Mrs Wodehouse rented Norma Shearer's and Irving Thalberg's house for a spell, and then Gayelord Hauser's house. The studio, in addition to paying him twenty-five hundred dollars a week when it picked up his option, permitted him to work at home – a tremendous boon, since both houses had splendid swimming pools. During his second stint in Hollywood, when he again worked on *Rosalie* – and this time it got made – the Wodehouses rented a house with a swimming pool next door to Nelson Eddy.

In the early twenties, whenever Wodehouse was working on Broadway shows he and his wife lived in Great Neck, then a woodsy village inhabited largely by literary and theatrical people; later on, they took to staying in the city – at the Fourteen Hotel, a small residential hotel at 14 East Sixtieth Street. As for their sojourns in France, one year in the early thirties they rented a country house in the hill town of Auribeau, twelve miles behind Cannes. They both adored the place, but when they got around to buying a house in France, the next year, they settled on one in Le Touquet, because of its ideal situation – two hours from England by boat and two and a half hours from Paris by train.

The Wodehouses now owned two houses, for in 1928 they had bought a London town house at 17 Norfolk Street, off Park Lane. (Leonora Rowley, Mrs Wodehouse's daughter by her first marriage, lived there with them until she married Peter Cazalet, a member of a prominent English mercantile and racing family. The Wodehouses had no children together.) The Norfolk Street house required a large staff: a butler, a footman, a cook, a scullery maid, two housemaids, and a parlour-maid, plus a chauffeur, who drove the Rolls-Royce. The butler had previously worked for a man of eminence, but Wodehouse found he liked the chauffeur better. This showed good judgement on his part, for the butler turned out to be a member of an underworld gang, and was sent to prison when he and his pals were caught attempting to hold up a shooting gallery. Only in London, and just for a short time there, did the Wodehouses live so grandly. Generally, they hired a couple to run their household. 'We had only one really exceptional servant,' Mrs Wodehouse said not long ago. 'He was a butler named Kreutz

– an Austrian – who was with us the year we lived in southern France. He had worked in embassies most of his life, because he had a naturally dignified manner and spoke half a dozen languages. Kreutz was a very, very nice man – nothing at all like those pompous butlers in my husband's books.'

Wherever Wodehouse happened to be hanging his hat or his bathing suit in the score of years between the two world wars, he worked constantly. Much as he enjoyed walking, swimming, and golfing, and dining with intelligent and congenial people, there was nothing he enjoyed more than writing. In addition to the multifarious other projects he was engaged in, between 1920 and 1935 he wrote, or collaborated in the writing of, twelve plays. These included *The Play's the Thing*, an adaptation of a comedy by Ferenc Molnár; *Good Morning, Bill*, an adaptation of a comedy by another Hungarian, Ladislaus Fodor; *By Candlelight*, an adaptation of a comedy by Siegfried Geyer, a Viennese playwright; and *Her Cardboard Lover*, an adaptation of Valerie Wyngate's adaptation of a French play by Jacques Deval. In that same period, he managed to bring out either a new novel or a new collection of short stories each year, and some years he brought out one of each. In the 1920s – before he fully realized how hard good plots are to come by and how zealously a novelist should husband them – he devoted a large portion of his time to short stories. For instance, he had written thirty-one short stories about Bertie Wooster and Jeeves before he threw his two stars together, in 1934, in their first novel, *Thank You, Jeeves*.

A considerable percentage of Wodehouse aficionados, by the way, believe that it is in the short story, and not in the novel, that he reached the summit of his art. One of the books of his that they prize most highly is *Ukridge*, a collection of ten stories, published in 1924, that marked the return to action of Stanley Featherstonehaugh Ukridge (pronounced Uke-ridge), whom Wodehouse had introduced back in 1906, in an uneven early novel called *Love Among the Chickens*. Ukridge, an absent-minded type who wears pince-nez that are held over his ears by the wire from a ginger-beer bottle, has never got his feet under him since the day he was expelled from Wrykyn. He is continually borrowing money or clothes from his friends – whom he addresses heartily as 'laddie' or 'old horse' – and continually devising outrageous schemes for making his fortune, prattling a steady obbligato all the while about how a man must have vision and the big, broad, flexible outlook. Nothing quite works out for Ukridge – and this is hardly a surprise to anyone, particularly the reader who remembers why Ukridge was expelled from Wrykyn: when he slipped out of school one night to attend a local fair he took care to disguise himself with a false beard, but forgot to remove his school cap. On the same high level as the stories about Ukridge are a number of golf stories that Wodehouse wrote in the early twenties. These were collected in two books, called in Britain *The Clicking of Cuthbert* and *The Heart of a Goof*, and in America *Golf Without Tears* and *Divots*. In the British editions, the setting is usually Marvis Bay, a low-pressure seaside resort, and in the American editions it is usually the Manhooset Golf and Country Club, but in both editions the stories are introduced and related by the Oldest Member, a sage who has seen it all many times before from his chair on the club veranda and is always ready to launch into an appropriate narrative for the benefit of any young member who is missing his pars in the great games of life and golf.

Having the Oldest Member on hand to supply the frame for the golf stories worked out very well for Wodehouse. One day in 1926, when he was waiting in Victoria

Station to board a train to Dulwich, he hit upon just the person he had been looking for to perform a comparable function whenever he had a wild and improbable tale to tell. This was Mr Mulliner, 'a short, stout, comfortable man of middle age', whose eyes held such childlike candour that you 'would have brought oil stock from him without a tremor'. Mr Mulliner's home course is a pub called the Anglers' Rest. No matter how arcane or offbeat the discussion under way in the bar parlour may be, you can count on Mr Mulliner to be reminded of a story that is very much to the point, for he has an inexhaustible supply of nephews, and one of them – perhaps Cyril Mulliner, the interior decorator, or George Mulliner, who has that terrible stammer, or Augustine Mulliner, the curate at Lower Briskett-in-the-Midden, or Adrian Mulliner, the detective, but in any event some young Mulliner – is bound to have undergone an amazing and light-shedding experience in that very province.

The average Wodehouse short story is about seventy-five hundred words long, and, counting the fees from both American and British magazines, the author was paid at the rate of about a dollar a word. Wodehouse felt that in a seventy-five-hundred-word story there should usually be two big socks, the first at around the fifteen-hundred-word mark and the second at around the six-thousand-word mark. After a while, it became second nature for him to construct his stories to that measure. Such classics of intricate design as 'Uncle Fred Flits By' and 'Strychnine in the Soup' demanded a little more time than most, but, as a rule, once Wodehouse had the plot of a short story thought out the actual writing took just about a week.

In the mid-thirties, after employing Wodehouse on other chores, Hollywood tardily discovered his own works. M-G-M made *Piccadilly Jim*, with Robert Montgomery and Madge Evans; RKO made *A Damsel in Distress*, with Fred Astaire and Joan Fontaine; and Twentieth Century-Fox made *Thank You, Jeeves* and *Step Lively, Jeeves*, with Arthur Treacher as Jeeves and David Niven as Bertie. The movie that came closest to capturing Wodehouse's distinctive ambience was *A Damsel in Distress*, possibly because the author assisted with the screenplay. As for the Jeeves pictures, their chief weakness was that Jeeves was presented as a caricature of a haughty stage butler, not as an essentially kindly valet. By that time – shortly before the outbreak of the Second World War – Wodehouse was far and away the most widely read writer of light fiction in the world. He was a special favourite of travellers, and no vacationer's equipment was considered complete unless he had a couple of Wodehouses tucked away along with his Agatha Christies. If he didn't, he could usually rectify the deficiency at the book counter on the railway platform when his train halted for ten minutes at Belfort, or Bologna, or wherever it was, for the chances were that some Wodehouse would be available, if not in a hard-cover edition, then in a Tauchnitz or Penguin paperback. Just before war broke out in 1939, the book that most of his admirers were talking about was *The Code of the Woosters*, in which Wodehouse and Wooster were at their best, tossing off one funny line after another. These, for instance:

He still remained the same galumphing man with two left feet, who had always been constitutionally incapable of walking through the great Gobi desert without knocking something over.

Madeline Bassett laughed the tinkling, silvery laugh which was one of the things that had got her so disliked by the better element.

He had played Rugby football not only for his University but also for England, and at the art of hurling an opponent into a mud puddle and jumping on his neck with cleated boots had had few, if any, superiors.

I had described Roderick Spoke to the butler as a man with an eye that could open an oyster at sixty paces.

Although the world that Wodehouse wrote about remained the same after the outbreak of war, the world he lived in changed drastically. Three unusual scenes come to mind when one thinks of Wodehouse and the war. The first is the eleventh-hour attempt that he and his wife made to get out of France after the Germans had broken through the French lines in the Ardennes. Up to that time, no one and nothing had been able to induce the Wodehouses to quit Le Touquet for the comparative safety of England; British regulations required animals entering the country to be quarantined for six months, and the Wodehouses, with their extravagant devotion to their dogs and cats, could not accept that idea. A few days before the German breakthrough, Lady Dudley, who, as Gertie Millar, had been a star of the English musical comedy stage, and who was Mrs Wodehouse's closest friend in Le Touquet, made a special trip back to France to try to convince the Wodehouses of the gravity of the situation, but she was unable to do so. Only when the vanguard of the German Army was sweeping across northern France did the Wodehouses move. Piling their pets into their Rolls-Royce, they headed for Abbeville in the wild hope of finding a boat that would carry them to England. The roads were impassable, clogged as they were by thousands of refugees fleeing before the invaders. There was nothing the Wodehouses could do but return that night to their home and await their capture.

The second scene is a smaller canvas: Wodehouse in the internment camp at Tost. In what is probably best described as the camp dayroom, he sits with a typewriter on his knees. There are perhaps fifty other prisoners in the room, some of them playing ping-pong or cards, others singing or talking. With his fantastic concentration, Wodehouse is thinking out and writing a new novel, *Money in the Bank*.

The third scene is one that was evoked by Malcolm Muggeridge in his spirited defence of Wodehouse's wartime conduct. 'Duff Cooper, as Minister of Information, led the pack against Wodehouse', Muggeridge wrote. 'In Paris, to his credit, he showed no inclination to follow up the attack with a kill. I was able to produce for him one instance of an authentic contribution by Wodehouse to the war effort. The Germans, in their literal way, took his works as a guide to English manners, and actually dropped an agent in the Fen country wearing spats. This unaccustomed article of attire led to his speedy apprehension. Had he not been caught, he would presumably have gone on to London in search of the Drones Club, and have thought to escape notice in restaurants by throwing bread about in the manner of Bertie.'

Remsenburg, where the Wodehouses lived, is an extraordinarily pretty Long Island village roughly halfway between Eastport and Westhampton Beach. No commercial establishments are permitted there, and, apart from a few churches and the post office, it is made up entirely of private homes, most of them white, modest, and simple. The Wodehouses came to know Remsenburg through Bolton, who had lived there since 1941. In 1952, when they were out visiting the Boltons, Ethel Wodehouse abruptly informed her husband at lunch one day, 'I bought a house here this morning.' At that time, the Wodehouses were living in New York, in a penthouse at 1000 Park Avenue, a duplex with a terrace large enough to accommodate several good-sized trees. For the next few years, they divided their time between the city and Long Island, but in 1959 they settled in Remsenburg for good, relinquishing the penthouse to Mignon G. Eberhardt, the mystery writer. By then, Mrs Wodehouse, a compulsive remodeller and redecorator, had knocked down several walls, extended the living room and the kitchen, added on a couple of sun parlours, and generally made their new quarters into a bright and cheerful, if digressive, house. She had then turned her attention to the ten nondescript adjoining acres, setting out gardens and installing a flowering tree here and a clump of shrubs there, until the land had the look of a proper English park. In another characteristic move, she provided twelve feeding stations for birds around the property.

When Mrs Wodehouse was entering her eightieth year, she and her husband were joined at Remsenburg by his brother Armine's widow, Nella, a pleasant and practical lady, who assumed a good deal of the responsibility for running the house. This left Mrs Wodehouse free to zip over in her car each day to the Westhampton branch of the Bide-a-Wee Home Association, where abandoned dogs and cats were cared for until they were ready for adoption. The branch, which opened in 1967, was later named the P. G. Wodehouse Shelter, after the major donor, who contributed thirty-five thousand dollars. The Wodehouses, by the way, decided not to give their house a name, but a number of Wodehouse readers decided, independently of each other, that it should be called Blandings Castle, and they addressed mail to him that way. Wodehouse received an average of three fan letters a day. They came from all over the world – a heartening percentage from young readers who had only just discovered him. 'Little need to say that we have been quite thoroughly infected by P. G.-osis', went a typical letter – this one from Istanbul. 'Having spotted *Galahad at Blandings* four months ago, one of us has read sixteen and the other fully twenty-four of your books. Devotedly yours, Ismi Tenikalp and Tomur Bayer.'

During his first few years in Remsenburg, Wodehouse took occasional breathers from his work to go in to New York to oversee some business matter or attend some social function like the Old Alleynians' annual dinner. Gradually his one-day trips to town became much less frequent, and then they ceased altogether. Two people in the city he continued to keep in close touch with were Scott Meredith, his American literary agent, and Peter

Schwed of Simon & Schuster, who was his American editor for a quarter of a century. Both men were Wodehouse fans long before they became associated with him, and both were devoted to him. Schwed, among his other services, kept Wodehouse in pipes, periodically sending him a favourite model – an Algerian briar with a huge pot-shaped bowl, made by Jobey. Schwed also kept him in raincoats. 'It seems that whenever Plum came to New York it turned out to be a rainy day, and invariably he'd forgotten to bring a raincoat,' Schwed told a friend not long ago. 'I made it a point to have one of those three- or four-dollar raincoats and some old hats in my office in case of emergency, and I must have outfitted Plum with a dozen of each. He did the same thing every time. He'd put on the cheap, crinkled raincoat and hat, study himself in the mirror, and say proudly, "My, very good-looking, isn't it?" '

Meredith whose first ambition was to become a Wodehouse-type writer, started to represent Wodehouse when he not only was under a cloud because of his wartime broadcasts but was regarded in some quarters as a writer whose kind of humour was *passé*. As a matter of fact, the man who preceded Meredith as Wodehouse's American agent held this opinion and told him so. 'When Wodehouse came over to us, he sent us two short stories that his previous agent had informed him were unsaleable,' Meredith recently recalled. 'I sent them on to Dale Eunson at *Cosmopolitan*, and he bought them both. Those two sales seemed to give Plum the lift and confidence he needed to get rolling again, and soon, I'm happy to say, we entered that period when he was being accepted back into the fold. His productive capacity never ceased to amaze me. In 1967, I told him just before Christmas that I had three magazine assignments for him – two light essays and one short story. I explained that they had to be in by early January, and asked him how many of the assignments he wanted to take on. He told me he thought he could handle the lot. And he did. They were all done by New Year's Day – vintage Wodehouse, too.' Wodehouse, for his part, was devoted to Schwed and Meredith. He declared his gratitude to them on numerous occasions, but, for good measure, knowing they would get a kick out of it, he regularly dropped their names into his novels. In *Ice in the Bedroom*, for instance, there is a scene in which a detective reassures a nervous client by saying, 'I shall have some of my best men with me – Meredith, certainly, and possibly Schwed.'

Wodehouse did his writing in his study – a fairly large, pine-walled room on the ground floor, overlooking the back garden. The principal pieces of furniture were a leather armchair (for lounging and thinking) and a plain wooden desk about three feet by five. On top of the desk were a dictionary, a knife for cleaning out pipes, and a bulky Royal typewriter, which Wodehouse had used since 1934. His method of composition remained virtually unchanged through the years. He did his first draft in longhand, in pencil. Then he sat down at the Royal and did a moderate amount of revising and polishing when he typed it. His average output on a good working day was about a thousand words in his last twenty years, but when he was younger it was closer to two thousand five hundred. He had his most productive day in 1933, when, to his own astonishment, he knocked off the final eight thousand words of *Thank You, Jeeves*. Once, when he was beginning a Wooster–Jeeves novel, he experimented with using a dictaphone. After he had dictated the equivalent of a page, he played it back to check it over. What he heard sounded so terribly unfunny that he immediately turned off the machine and went back to his pad and pencil.

Wodehouse also did most of his reading in his study. On shelves on the wall facing his desk he had assembled a copy of each of the ninety-odd books he had written, and the books of his favourite authors lined the adjacent walls – among them nine books by George Ade, seven by W. W. Jacobs, twenty-two by Barry Pain, seven by Robert Benchley, eleven by Cyril Hare, thirty-six by Patricia Wentworth, sixteen by A. A. Milne, fourteen by Henry Cecil, ten by Robert Barr, nine by F. Anstey, eight by Ngaio Marsh, and the complete works of Shakespeare, which he re-read every two or three years. (In his opinion, Shakespeare's most underrated play was *Love's Labour's Lost*.) The library also contained all the books of Colette, Anthony Powell, James Thurber, Evelyn Waugh, E. B. White, Rex Stout, and Agatha Christie. Over the last half century of his life Wodehouse read something like a hundred and fifty mystery novels annually, and he had a pretty clear idea whom he would rank as the top five writers in that realm – Dame Agatha, Stout, Dame Ngaio, Miss Wentworth, and Hare, in about that order. He believes that what gives Agatha Christie's books their peculiar fascination is that 'no one is safe – anyone can be the murderer'. Although he and Dame Agatha never met, she was well aware that Wodehouse was one of her most steadfast admirers, and she dedicated one of her books, *Hallowe'en Party*, to him.

Chief among the attractions that a first-class mystery holds for Wodehouse is its necessarily sound and well-joined plot. Unlike most literary humorists, who tend to regard the story line as merely a means of setting their funny stuff in motion, Wodehouse has always been obsessed with making each twist and turn in a novel or a short story as watertight as the seams of an Indian canoe. Before he sets down one word of his manuscript, he prepares a detailed scenario – an arduous process that may require from two to three months to complete, and occasionally much longer. Putting his thoughts down on paper helps him clarify his thinking, so when he is developing a scenario he jots down daily the ideas that are going through his mind about the section of the plot he is currently concerned with. For instance, if he introduces a new character at this point, will that fix the trouble he's encountering with the love story? Did he dawdle too long before getting into things, and should he start over again and introduce all the principal characters in the first chapter? Is that first major scene wrong because it comes too early or because the heroine – face it – is dull and upsympathetic? Such conversations with himself can run to considerable length. When Wodehouse was blocking out *Bill the Conqueror*, for instance, it took him thirteen thousand words to reach the halfway point in his outline for a novel that was itself only eighty thousand words long.

Because of the exertion that goes into his scenarios, the actual writing of his novels is usually smooth sailing. There have been a few storm-tossed exceptions, however. The first thirty thousand words of the first draft of *Leave It to Psmith* had to be scrapped, because the scenario didn't hold up. The first thirty thousand words of each of the first three drafts of *Hot Water* had to be scrapped before the story satisfied him. *Big Money* was even worse; whole sections of the beginning, the middle, and the end of the book had to be rewritten three times. *The Luck of the Bodkins* was another backbreaker. Wodehouse explained in a letter about that novel to an old Dulwich classmate, William Townend, 'I had such a good farcical plot in this one that I got all hopped up and felt it wasn't possible to give 'em too much of this superb stuff, so every scene I wrote was elaborated until it lost its grip.' Wodehouse put the manuscript aside temporarily and then, when he returned to it, cut twenty-five thousand words. That helped, but didn't cure all the ailments of *The Luck of the Bodkins*, a novel that has the odd distinction of reaching its peak in its opening sentence:

Into the face of the young man who sat on the terrace of the Hotel Magnifique at Cannes there had crept a look of furtive shame, the shifty, hangdog look which announces that an Englishman is about to talk French.

For all his discipline and his passion for order, Wodehouse was no different from other writers in that from time to time he stopped work on a troublesome story and turned his attention to some other project that was coming to a boil after a lengthy period of simmering, but he was a tenacious man, and more often than not he would keep returning to an idea until he found himself ready to apply the full force of his imagination and technical skill to it and bring it to a successful conclusion. A case in point is one of his last novels, *The Girl in Blue*. Wodehouse started to think about *The Girl in Blue* on 28 September 1951, nearly twenty years before the book came out. On that day, he broke ground by writing:

Central Idea: The rich American who is a kleptomaniac.

I can see the start of the story – a family council like the one in Elmer Rice's *Imperial City*. The family has assembled to decide what is to be done about Uncle Joe, who is very rich but who has this unfortunate habit of sneaking things, and they have only just – by bribery and corruption – got him out of being charged with shoplifting at Macy's or some other store. They are socially prominent and shudder at the thought of any scandal. So what to do? They decide to send him to England in charge of hero – who is hero? – or heroine – who is heroine? – because they feel that if he gets pinched in England, it won't lead to publicity.

For three pages, Wodehouse explored some thoughts

about his hero and heroine and about possible incidents that might trigger the plot. He then dropped the scenario, and twenty months passed before he returned to it. That was on 14 June 1953, when he began another three pages of notes by writing:

Story So Far –
We start with a family council in New York – very posh, rich family, very starchy. Aunt Jane is kleptomaniac, and they have only just succeeded in getting her out of being charged with shop-lifting, she having pinched some stuff at a jeweller's. They are socially prominent and shudder at thought of scandal. What to do? They decide that son of family shall take her to England and deposit her in the wilds of the country somewhere, where she can't get into trouble – and if she does it won't lead to publicity.

Wodehouse then forgot about this novel for three more years. He went back to the scenario on 31 August 1956, writing a single page of notes, which started like this:

Try it another way. On lines of Bill the Conqueror. Hero is in America, in love with haughty girl. She has a brother who is a kleptomaniac and she makes hero take him over to England and keep an eye on him. Or possibly better, Brother is a susceptible young man and is in constant danger of marrying a chorus girl.

No, I don't think so. Whatever peculiarity Brother has should lead to complications – such as stealing something. Is there anything to be got out of making him a firebug – see story by Evelyn Waugh in that book of stories which I have – and owner of old country house somehow finds this out and invites hero and Brother to house. In other words, make it like Fiery Wooing of Mordred.

This was followed by another long hiatus, which ended on 24 May 1958. On that date, he returned to the scenario, adding two pages of notes, including the following variations on the original theme:

Try this. Hero runs Big Brother agency or whatever it is called. Fiancée wants him to give it up and go into business. He doesn't want to, as it is fun. When kleptomaniac pinches whatever it is, Fiancée's father (or Uncle Cedric) comes to agency to commission it to recover this.

Just as suddenly as he had taken the scenario up again, he suspended work on it. He had better fish to fry. He did not give another thought to Uncle Cedric & Co. – or, at least, he added nothing to the existing scenario – for more than seven years. Then, on 3 January 1966, he went back to it. He wrote a page of notes that day, two pages on 4 January, two more pages on 5 January, and six pages on 7 January. That long entry on 7 January began:

Story So Far —
Two families are involved – (a) In New York, an aristocratic New York family – call them the X's, (b) In England, a hard-up aristocratic family, the Y's, who consist of Cedric, who owns the castle, his daughter A, and his niece B.

The story opens in New York. A family council is going on. C, an aunt, has been caught shoplifting and the family, headed by D, a very correct, starchy young man, are discussing what to do with her. They have squared this last charge, but she may slip again and there will be a scandal.

Wodehouse's interest in the story had been rekindled. For the next five weeks, he toiled away at the scenario almost daily. By 4 February, he had refined his story line and settled on the following cast of characters:

1 – Owner of castle. Hypochondriac.
2 – His daughter. Domineering.
3 – His niece (heroine).
4 – His brother-in-law. Millionaire financier.
5 – Low X. (Hero.) Hard-up. Writes detective stories.
6 – Starchy young American. Very proud of his family.
7 – His aunt. Kleptomaniac.

8 – Chimp Twist. Private detective. Crook.
9 – Heroine's fiancé. An MP stuffed shirt.

About a week after this, however, work on the scenario slammed to a halt. Before Wodehouse returned to *The Girl in Blue* again – this time to see it through to its conclusion – it was 1969, and he had finished two other novels, *Do Butlers Burgle Banks?* and *A Pelican at Blandings* (American title: *No Nudes is Good Nudes*). In the final version of *The Girl in Blue*, Mrs Bernadette Clayborne, the rich widowed sister of Homer Pyle, an eminent New York corporation lawyer, has been arrested for shoplifting at Guildenstern's, a big Madison Avenue department store. Fortunately, the manager of Guildenstern's is an old college friend of Pyle's, and he agrees not to prefer charges against Mrs Clayborne, provided Pyle gets her out of the city immediately. Pyle does better than that – he gets her out of the country. It seems that Willoughby Scrope, a London lawyer who is a good friend of Pyle's, has a brother named Crispin, who runs Mellingham Hall, a fine old country house that takes paying guests and is situated miles from the nearest department store. Pyle, who is on his way to Brussels to attend a PEN conference – he writes poetry on the side – drops his sister off with Willoughby Scrope, who, it happens, has just brought off a great coup: he has just acquired, at an auction at Sotheby's, a miniature Gainsborough called 'The Girl in Blue', which he had been trying to track down for years. It seems that . . .

One day early in 1971, two men who were old friends and admirers of Wodehouse's, and who lived in New York City and had not seen him for some time, arranged to pay him a brief visit in Remsenburg. Since they were not due before noon, Wodehouse adhered to his regular morning schedule: after the daily dozen and breakfast, he went into his study at nine o'clock and put in a couple of hours at his desk. He was in exceptionally good spirits, partly because he was looking forward to seeing his friends and going out to lunch with them but mainly because he was once again embarked upon a novel – yet another instalment in the saga of Bertie Wooster and Jeeves. Wodehouse, like his readers, had become deeply attached to them, and the hard work of roughing out the scenario had so far presented few problems. That morning he was wearing the gold-blue-and-white-striped tie of the Warwickshire County Cricket Club. Just prior to the First World War, a bowler named Jeeves played for Warwickshire, and Wodehouse happened to remember him a few years later when he was searching for a good offbeat name for an omniscient valet. In recognition of this happy circumstance, the WCCC had sent Wodehouse a club tie, and it saw considerable service.

In the interval before his friends appeared, Wodehouse went through his morning mail. It included two fan letters relayed by his publisher and a long, warm letter from Kreutz, the Wodehouses' old butler, who had retired and was living in Bad Homburg. Wodehouse then dipped into the airmail edition of the *Sunday Times*, which he got each week, along with the airmail edition of the *Observer*. The one other periodical he subscribed to was *Punch*. Like the characters in his books, he had changed hardly at all over the years, and although it might be going a bit too far to describe the life that he and his wife led as Edwardian, it did smack of an earlier, gentler era, and it was very English. Their eating habits were a case in point: a kipper frequently appeared on Wodehouse's luncheon tray; tea was served every afternoon; and the evening meal featured solid, dependable stuff like roast lamb with mint sauce and roast potatoes. Despite Wodehouse's many years in America, his speech did not show the slightest trace of an American accent or intonation. The voice was faintly nasal and rather high in pitch, like Reginald Owen's; the sentences were swung out with a measured cadence that was almost a lilt; the vocabulary was that of Wodehouse's youth, when a fellow was a 'chap' and a serious argument was a 'frightful row'. Equally English was the fact that the Wodehouses' four dogs – a dachshund called Jed, a Pekingese called Boy, a 'collie-type' called Minnie, and a boxer called Debbie – had the run of the house, along with five cats, Ginger, Baby, Smokie, Cookie and Blackie.

Wodehouse's friends arrived a few minutes after twelve. He led the way to the back sun parlour, where Mrs Wodehouse joined them for a moment before rushing off to the Bide-a-Wee shelter with a large package of bones. The men exchanged personal news, and Wodehouse fetched a proof of a dust jacket he had just received from his American publisher, after which he collected his walking stick and tracked down his new checked cap from Lock's – it had been resting on a chair in the corner of the living room where his colour prints of Dulwich College are hung – and the party drove to the Patio. His two friends ordered Martinis; Wodehouse, a bourbon sour 'straight up'. This seemed to whet his appetite; in any event, he polished off a cup of jellied madrilène, an order of lamb stew, a side order of stringbeans, several hard rolls, a salad, a biscuit Tortoni, and a cup of coffee.

Near the beginning of the lunch, apropos of nothing previously discussed, he asked his friends, 'I say, could a chap who's just run for Parliament and won his seat suddenly chuck it all, just like that?' His friends didn't see why not. Wodehouse explained that he was thinking of using this situation in the new Bertie Wooster novel. 'It will be very much like the earlier Bertie and Jeeves novels,' he said. 'I don't know if that is a good thing or not. For years, I've got letters from readers asking me why I persist in writing so many country-house novels. That has always surprised me. I know that when I read one of Rex Stout's Nero Wolfe mysteries I'm terribly disappointed if it doesn't take place in his home on Thirty-fifth Street. The last Nero Wolfe I read was set on a dude ranch out West. I missed the orchids – the whole New York atmosphere, which Rex Stout does so well. No, I hardly think it would be an improvement if I were to write a novel laid in Yugoslavia or the Crimea.'

During lunch, Wodehouse – a man who has always abhorred people who hold forth – kept trying to switch the conversation to his friends. It inevitably returned to him and his work, for that was what his friends wanted to talk about. Over coffee, one of them asked him if the world he wrote about had really ever existed.

'Oh, it very definitely existed,' Wodehouse replied with animation. 'When I was living in London around the turn of the century, a good many of the young men dressed in morning coats, toppers, and spats – or spatterdashes, to give them their full name. I wore them myself when I paid afternoon calls. I don't know why spats went out of favour. They were very comfortable, you know. Awfully warm. Anyway, when I started writing my stories, Bertie was a recognizable type. All the rich young men had valets.' He paused for a moment or so, then said, 'Funny how fast a type disappears! After the war, there wasn't nearly so much money around, so the young men had to go out and find jobs, and this sort of pulled the rug out from under a whole way of life. Now my stories read like historical novels. I imagine there must be quite a few aspects of my stuff which the new generation of readers doesn't begin to understand. Let me put it this way. When I was a boy reading all those Greek and Latin authors, the one who appealed to me most was Aristophanes. He was a very funny fellow. But, you know, he must have seemed ever so much funnier to the Greeks. That is the point I want to make. I suppose we miss eighty per cent of Aristophanes' humour. Some line that means nothing much to us might have been a wonderful dig at Cleon.'

On many days, Guy Bolton used to pick Wodehouse up at around two o'clock and they would go for their walk down the neighbourhood lanes. On this particular afternoon, the walk had been cancelled – Bolton had been summoned to New York to discuss a possible production of his new play, *A Man and His Wife*, which was about Winston and Clementine Churchill. Consequently, there was no need for Wodehouse to be home before three-thirty when the television serial, 'The Edge of Night', went on. By that time, his friends were on their way back to the city and he was in his armchair in front of the television set in his study. For many years, it was his habit to watch another soap opera, 'Love of Life', which went on at noon, but when a new man started writing the script for the show, it lost its appeal for Wodehouse. He greatly admired Henry Slesar, the writer of 'The Edge of Night', and spoke of him as 'a chap who has a good story to tell and knows how to tell it'. Aside from this, the things he most liked to watch on television were the New York Mets' baseball games.

At the close of that day's instalment of 'The Edge of Night', Wodehouse fell off into a snooze. It was after five when he roused himself. He took a shower, changed his clothes, and went back to the armchair. As he was thinking out possible directions that the scenario of the new novel might take, Mrs Wodehouse called to him. He joined her in the back sun parlour, where she had set out two glasses of sherry. 'I'm going to watch the Mets' game tonight,' he told her. 'They're playing Pittsburgh.'

'I don't know what you see in baseball, Plummie,' she said. 'It's so dull.'

'Oh, it's a good game to watch,' he protested. 'A much better game to watch than cricket, Ethel. The trouble with cricket is that you're a Surrey fan, say, and the other team wins the toss – well, they come in and bat all day. You never see your team do a thing.'

'I should think you'd find American football more exciting than baseball,' Mrs Wodehouse said.

'Oh, not at all,' he answered. 'They run a play and then they all gather round and discuss it.'

There followed a stretch of silence, during which they both sipped their sherry and gazed at the back garden and the trees beyond.

'How nice it looks now, with the evening light on the lawn,' Wodehouse said.

≡ III ≡

Envoi

In the autumn of 1971, I drove out to Long Island to attend Wodehouse's ninetieth birthday party which was held at the Henry Perkins Hotel in the town of Riverhead, some nine miles from Remsenburg. I arrived at the hotel a little before six, just as Wodehouse was disembarking from his car. I was struck by how well he looked despite the constant interruptions to the tidy pattern of his life which he had been forced to put up with during the previous two weeks. For example, on many of the days preceding his birthday he got very little writing done, for he was kept so busy answering the phone and talking with interviewers that he was lucky to get to his desk at all. One day a large television crew from the BBC started shooting a 'typical Wodehouse day' at ten in the morning and didn't finish until ten at night. As a result, Wodehouse hadn't been able to do any of the things he did on a typical day.

About sixty people were on hand for the birthday party, which took place in the Windsor Room of the Henry Perkins. Most of them were friends of the Wodehouses from Remsenburg and the adjoining towns, but a few had driven out from New York City, among them Scott Meredith, Wodehouse's American agent, and Peter Schwed of Simon and Schuster, Wodehouse's American publisher. (Schwed had arranged for Wodehouse's new novel –

called *Jeeves and the Tie That Binds* in the United States, and *Much Obliged, Jeeves* in Great Britain – to be published on his birthday, and one of the presents he carried out was a leather-bound copy of the book.) The Windsor Room had a rather festive aura. In the dance-floor area, in the centre of the room, a small combo – a piano player and a girl singer who used wire brushes to play a stand-up type of drum known as a cocktail drum – was running through 'Blue Skies', 'I Get a Kick Out of You', and other tunes from the 1920s and 1930s. A number of photographers were circling around, filling the air with the flashes of bulbs. Wodehouse, who had settled himself in a wing chair at one side of the room, sipped a Scotch-and-soda as he welcomed his friends. There was, I noticed, hardly a trace of wrinkles in his pinkish face, and his blue eyes were twinkling brightly. He looked nothing like his age. He was dressed in a tan jacket, brown trousers, an off-white shirt, a gold tie with some pale striping, and brown loafers with brass buckles. When I told him how contemporary he looked, he asked if I thought the tie was all right. 'I wanted to wear my Warwickshire County Cricket Club tie,' he said. 'Just before the First World War, a chap named Jeeves used to bowl for Warwickshire. That's where I got the name. I must have mentioned that to you. Anyhow, the club tie is a real beauty – gold and blue and white stripes. I wanted to wear it tonight, but Ethel said this tie went much better with my outfit, and there you are.'

Mrs Wodehouse, a slim, energetic woman, who is a few years younger than her husband, had on a filmy culotte dress and was circulating briskly among the guests. 'It's been absolutely hectic,' she told me. 'The phone hasn't stopped ringing for days. Guy and Virginia Bolton called from London. My grandchildren, Edward Cazalet and Sharon Hornby, also called from England, and I can't tell you how many people have phoned from all over. And the wires! I think Plummie's received well over a hundred. Agatha Christie sent one. Basil Boothroyd of *Punch*. Terence Rattigan. The headmaster of Plummie's old school, Dulwich, sent one, and so did the Dulwich Cricket Club. Those two really meant a lot to him. Of course, the mail has been impossible. Sacks of it! Over three hundred birthday cards so far, and all kinds of presents – everything, literally, from a tuning fork to a jar of bramble jelly. It's been wonderful but hectic. One time when the phone rang this afternoon, Plummie looked over and asked, "Has the Queen called yet?" '

Just before everyone sat down to dinner, I had a chat with Nella Wodehouse, the widow of the writer's older brother Armine. She had helped run the house the past seven years. 'We all took it slowly today,' she said. 'Plummie slept late for him, and had a very light lunch – some fillets of flounder and some cheese and biscuits. Then he watched his favourite television serial, "The Edge of Night". He's become a good friend of the man who writes it, Henry Slesar – he's the tall chap over there. Well, it was a good thing Plummie didn't miss it today. There was a scene where a rather elderly man is reading a newspaper, and another character asks him what's in the news. "Nothing much," the man says. "There's another hurricane forming in the Caribbean and . . . Ah, here's some good news: This is P. G. Wodehouse's ninetieth birthday. That fellow's been making me laugh for fifty years." When Plummie heard that, he almost jumped out of his chair.'

There were some pleasant interruptions during dinner. At one point, the two musicians moved into a charming arrangement of 'Bill', from *Show Boat*, and almost instantly a hush fell over the room; everyone seemed to know that Wodehouse had written the lyric, which is probably his most famous one. At another point, Wode-house was prevailed upon to open one of his presents, which was in a box about three feet wide and two feet high. A gift from Scott Meredith, it proved to be a huge leather pig, to be used as a footrest, and as it emerged from the wrapping paper, the guests, obviously conversant with all of Wodehouse's characters, called out as one man, 'The Empress of Blandings!' Later, after Wodehouse had been toasted in champagne, there was a brief scene right out of one of his novels. In those days the bulk of Mrs Wodehouse's free time went to the Bide-a-Wee animal shelter in Westhampton, and the birthday proceedings were momentarily sidetracked when, at her insistence, a gentleman from Bide-a-Wee headquarters, in New York, stepped to the microphone and, sparing no details, brought everyone up to date on the organization's activities.

After dinner, and just before the party broke up, I had another chat with Wodehouse. He seemed pleased when I told him how well he looked. 'I *have* been feeling well,' he said. 'However, whenever you go to a doctor, they never tell you what's wrong with you. They wrap that rubber contraption around your arm and inflate it, and then they yell out some scores.' He paused to relight his cigar. 'Life is complicated, isn't it? Here I am longing to get back to work on my new novel. It's a sort of sequel to *The Luck of the Bodkins*, and it's been going extremely well. The trouble is it may take weeks before I finish acknowledging all the birthday cards and telegrams. I don't know if Ethel or Nella told you, but I received an awfully nice telegram from Richard Burton and Elizabeth Taylor. I had no idea they were fans of mine. What I'm wondering about now is how one goes about answering them. Does one simply start off, "Dear Richard and Elizabeth"? Complicated stuff.'

A middle-aged couple came over to say good night. When they had gone on, Wodehouse resumed our talk. 'I'm delighted to have reached ninety,' he said. 'But then, the Wodehouses *are* a long-lived family. As I must have told you, my grandfather fought at Waterloo. That's a hundred and fifty-six years ago. I find that impressive.'

When his ninetieth birthday party was behind him, Wodehouse quickly returned to his customary daily routine. There was no diminuendo in the amount of work he steadily produced. The sequel to *The Luck of the Bodkins* was published in Great Britain under the title *Pearls, Girls, and Monty Bodkin* in 1972 and in the United States as *The Plot That Thickened* in 1973. *Bachelors Anonymous*, a very dexterous performance, appeared in Britain in 1973 and in the States the following year. Close on its heels came a high-spirited Jeeves–Wooster novel called *Aunts Aren't Gentlemen* in Britain and *The Cat-nappers* in the States. It was brought out in 1974 by its British publisher and in 1975 by its American publisher.

It is not uncommon for writers – novelists especialy – to lose a little of the spin on the ball as they grow older, but this wasn't true in Wodehouse's case. He wrote with as much freshness and command in his nineties as he had sixty years before when he first cracked the *Saturday Evening Post* and shortly thereafter became a best-selling author in both Britain and America. His daily stint of writing and thinking out future projects had always given him pleasure and a feeling of accomplishment, and in his later years the sense of continuity he derived from his work was important. He was much too modest ever to say it in so many words, but it was intensely gratifying to him that the adventures of Bertie, Lord Emsworth, Mr Mulliner, Psmith, and the other residents of the demesne he had created were read with ardour and delight by the grandchildren of the first generation of Wodehouse enthusiasts.

Although he had become an American citizen in 1955, Wodehouse also retained his British citizenship. In the 1975 New Year's Honours list, Queen Elizabeth conferred a knighthood on him. One cannot overstate how much this meant to Wodehouse. His knighthood not only recognized his immense literary achievements, but it signified that he had been welcomed back proudly into the family. No more would he be besieged by thoughts that in Britain he might still be regarded in some quarters as a man who had let his country down in the Second World War. Some of Wodehouse's friends are of the opinion that what kept him going during the last decades of his life was the ever-flickering hope that he would be knighted and that this would bring to an end once and for all the unfortunate Wodehouse Affair. They may well be right. Six weeks or so after receiving his knighthood, Wodehouse died. The date was 14 February 1975. He was ninety-three.

Wodehouse died in a hospital in Remsenburg of a heart attack. As Richard Usborne, the Wodehouse scholar, has put it, he was at work till the end. He had taken to the hospital with him sixteen typed first-draft chapters of a new Blandings novel and thirty-three handwritten pages of notes, outlines, and general thoughts on that novel. In his hospital room, he did some work on the book the last day of his life.

Index

Ade, George, 67
Ainslee's, 44
Aldwych Theatre, 39
Alleynian, The (Dulwich College school magazine), 35, 36
American Society of Composers, Authors, and Publishers, 52
Angler's Rest, the, 59
Anstey, F., 43, 67
Answers, 37
Argosy, 44
'Artistic Career of Corky, The', 54
Asquith, Herbert, 20
Aunts, 23, 33, 34, 37
Aunts Aren't Gentlemen (1974) (= *The Cat-nappers* [1975] in America), 85

Baboo Jabberjee (F. Anstey), 43
Bachelors Anonymous (1973), 85
Baldwin, Stanley, 20
Balfour, Arthur, 20
Barr, Robert, 67
Barrie & Jenkins, 53
  Autograph Edition of PGW's Books, 53
Baseball (New York Mets'), 15, 77

Bassett, Madeline, 23, 60
Beach (the butler), 46
Begbie, Harold, 37, 38
Beiderbecke, Bix, 20
Bellec, Hilaire, 21
Benchley, Robert, 67
Big Money (1931), 68
'Bill' (in *Show Boat*), 50, 83–4
Bill the Conqueror (1924), 68
Blandings Castle, 23, 27, 46, 86
Bolton, Guy, 13, 27, 28, 31, 48, 49, 50, 51, 55, 63, 76, 82
  Virginia, 28, 82
Bostock, Hermione, 23
Brinkley Court, 23
Burke's Peerage, 32
Burton, Richard, 84
By Candlelight, 57
'By the Way' (column of the *Globe*), 37, 38
Byng, Stiffy, 23

Carte, Rupert D'Oyly, 41, 42
Caryll, Felix (Ivan), 50
Cecil, Henry, 67
Chalmers, William FitzWilliam Delamere (= Lord Dawlish), 46
Christie, Agatha, 21, 60, 67, 83

'Wonderful stuff. Can you lend me five hundred pounds, Bodkin?'

As one of the only two really moneyed men at the Drones Club — Oofy Prosser was the other — Monty had often been given ample opportunity, coming to the rescue of financially embarrassed friends and acquaintances, and their urge to share his wealth had never occasioned astonishment. But this was the first time a multi-millionaire ~~had~~ ~~been~~ ~~touched~~ ~~by~~ (had expressed the desire to get into his ruts,) he gazed at Mr Llewellyn with eyes widening to the size of regulation golf balls.

'Five hundred pounds?' he quavered.

Mr.d's manner betrayed ~~a touch of~~ a touch of impatience.

~~or a thousand, if you'd rather~~ "You must have got it, dammit. A thousand dollars a week I am paying you for a year at the studio. You can't have spent it all.'

'No, no. I've got it.'

'And you'll let me have it?'

'Of course, of course!'

'Good boy, Bodkin. I always liked you, though you may have been deceived at times by my surface manner. Would it run to a thousand pounds?'

'Certainly, only too pleased.

'That's the sort of thing I like to hear. You have your checkbook with you?'

'Oh, yes.'

'Then perhaps? --- No time like the present!